Intermezzo

Household Matters

Wisteria Tearoom Mysteries

A Fatal Twist of Lemon
A Sprig of Blossomed Thorn
An Aria of Omens
A Bodkin for the Bride
A Masquerade of Muertos
As Red As Any Blood
A Black Place and a White Place
A Valentine for One

Intermezzi (Interludes)

Intermezzo: Spirit Matters
to be read between books 5 and 6
Intermezzo: Family Matters
to be read between books 6 and 7
Intermezzo: Household Matters
to be read between books 7 and 8

The Intermezzi are not mysteries, nor are they full-length
novels. They are interludes, shorter stories about the
series characters.

*I*NTERMEZZO

*H*OUSEHOLD *M*ATTERS

A Wisteria Tearoom Interlude

Patrice Greenwood

Evennight Books
Cedar Crest, New Mexico

This is a work of fiction. All of the characters, organizations, and events portrayed in this novel are either products of the author's imagination or are used fictitiously.

INTERMEZZO: HOUSEHOLD MATTERS

Evennight Books
P.O. Box 1644
Cedar Crest, NM 87008-1644

evennight.com

Cover photo: Pati Nagle

ISBN: 978-1-952653-03-2

First Edition July 2021

for Vivien,
who wears the best hats

Acknowledgments

My thanks to Deborah Ross and Chris Krohn for their help with this book, and to all my buddies in the Treehouse (treehousewriters.com) for their support and encouragement.

A Note from the Author

Dear Readers,

This book is a little different. I'd like to explain a few things so you'll know what to expect.

~ This is not a mystery. The next Wisteria Tearoom Mystery is *A Valentine for One*.

~ This is not a novel. It's a novella, about a third as long as a novel, yet it is a complete story. It is short and sweet. That's why it costs less than the novels.

~ This is not "leftovers." It is not text that was edited out of a novel. It's all original material that is focused on the characters in the series.

~ Where it fits: this story falls between book 7, *A Black Place and a White Place*, and book 8, *A Valentine for One*.

~ Finally, if you have not encountered the Wisteria Tearoom books before, this is not the best one to start with. Any of the mysteries—the full-length novels—is a better choice. Since they're sequential, I recommend starting with book 1, *A Fatal Twist of Lemon*.

I hope you enjoy this little interlude. Meanwhile, I'm off to the writing chair to work on book 8.

—Patrice Greenwood

1

I STOOD BACK, LOOKING AT THE TWO CHARMING ALCOVES we were about to destroy, and couldn't help feeling a sense of loss. Poppy and Hyacinth were both small—the smallest alcoves in the tearoom, accommodating only two guests in each—but parties of two were a large part of our business and I had worked to make both of these seatings beautiful. Poppy had cheerful red chairs, a sweet little standing lamp with a red beaded shade, and a black lacquer oriental screen with red peonies and gold cranes. Hyacinth's chairs were a dreamy, soft blue, complemented by tap-estry screens of lush blue and lavender flowers. In my heart, I didn't want to give them up.

You'll increase the square footage of the gift shop by half, said Kris's voice in my head. *And you'll get rid of that pass-through in Poppy. It's a win.*

The pass-through was awkward, true. Parties in Poppy had to put up with people stepping through to the two alcoves beyond it, Dahlia and Violet. But no one had ever complained.

My Aunt Nat, who had helped me set it all up months ago, gave me a knowing smile. "It's hard, isn't it? So many memories."

I nodded. The tearoom had been open less than a year, but there were many good memories. And some not so good, of course. Life was like that.

"Let's go, *hija*," said Uncle Manny, leaning on the hand truck he'd brought from his delivery truck. "I want to catch a game this afternoon."

Sighing, I let go. Farewell, Hyacinth and Poppy. I had photographs to remember them by. This wasn't the first change we had made to the tearoom's seatings, and it would doubtless not be the last.

"Screens first," I said. "Take them upstairs, please."

Manny stepped forward, carefully lifting the lacquer screen away from the furnishings of Poppy and folding it before carrying it away. I picked up an empty storage box and set it on one of the red chairs. Nat brought tissue paper over from the sales counter, and we began carefully wrapping the ornaments on the tables and putting them in the box.

Nat picked up a poppy-bedecked teapot that had long ago lost its lid and was now serving as a vase. The white lilies and red carnations it held were beginning to fade. I watched with a twinge of possessiveness as she carried it over to the sales counter. Glancing at the framed print of a painting of poppies that hung on the wall beside the fireplace, I decided to keep it there, in honor of Poppy. Same with the print of hyacinths on the other side.

It was a good business decision, I reminded myself for the zillionth time. It would improve our cash flow. But I would still miss these alcoves. Money was nice, but it wasn't cozy.

We finished packing the ornaments in short order. I gazed sadly at the empty tables.

"Where do you want the lamp?" Nat asked, unplugging the standing lamp from the discreet power strip tucked against the cupboard that had divided the two alcoves.

"In the hall, by the foot of the stairs. We'll put the chairs there, too."

"All of them?"

"Just the red ones."

I hadn't decided what to do with the chairs from Hyacinth. I didn't want the hall to get too cluttered, and we already had the gold chairs from Marigold-that-was sitting by the front door.

I paused, remembering the Room of Many Chairs at Ghost Ranch, and had to smile. No, we would not have the Hall of Many Chairs here. The blue chairs would go upstairs, facing the television I had recently unearthed from storage, and the tapestry screens would separate them from the sitting area by the front window. The upper hall was gradually becoming my living room, an extension of my suite.

Except that I wouldn't be living here much longer. Tony and I still needed to find a place. The clock was quietly ticking away the seconds before the wedding. We needed to find a venue for that, too.

One thing at a time, I told myself, and opened the doors of the waist-high cupboard that stood between Poppy and Hyacinth as a divider and support for one of the tapestry screens. I removed a couple of boxes of gift shop inventory and set them on the sales counter. The cupboard would go upstairs, too, replacing the storage boxes that were currently holding the TV.

It didn't take long at all. Manny hauled the furniture upstairs, and Nat got out the vacuum and gave the oriental rug a good going-over before I rolled it and took it upstairs as well. Returning to the gift shop, I stood in the doorway to appreciate the newly opened space. The wood floor gleamed, and the room felt less cramped.

We would fill the space, of course—with a second table of inventory to match the existing one, and two more display cabinets along the south wall. Manny had it all in his van outside: the cabinets and two matching credenzas, which would go back-to-back to form the table, along with a board cut to fit on top of them.

The room would still have a more open quality, though, and I liked that. The credenzas would provide more storage for inventory, and shoppers would have more to choose from. They would also be able to enjoy the fireplace that the two alcoves had shared, each having only a partial view.

Looking at the fireplace now, I shivered and thought about making a fire. It was a cold day, and Manny had propped the front door open so he could bring in the new furniture.

"Come on," Nat said, grabbing my hand and pulling me toward the now-unobstructed doorway to Dahlia. She led me through to Violet, where a cozy-covered teapot and two cups rested on the table between the two chairs. Nat pointed to the chair by the window with a commanding finger, and I obeyed. She took the other chair, lifted the cozy, and poured tea for us both.

"When did you make this?" I asked.

"While you were upstairs arranging the

furniture."

"Thank you," I said, warming my hands around the cup. It was oolong, a tea that demanded one relax and pay attention. I loved that the French called it *thé bleu,* "blue tea." I inhaled the steam, fragrant with a hint of oxidation, then let out a long breath and leaned back in the wing chair.

"It'll be splendid," Nat said. "You'll see."

"I know it will be. I'm just a little worried about losing the seatings. We're nearly booked up for the week of Valentine's Day."

"Didn't Kris say the open seating in the dining parlor would make up for it?"

"Yes."

In December, we had offered cream tea in the dining parlor on a first come, first served basis, and it had been a big success. Shoppers without reservations had been able to relax with tea and scones at the large dining table, with the only exceptions being times when the room had been booked for afternoon tea by a private party. But we didn't get all that many big parties, and the dining parlor would have stood empty if not for the cream tea. Kris had done the math, and even with the lower price of cream tea, the flow-through and the higher capacity for guests (the table could seat up to ten) had more than equaled the revenue from Poppy and Hyacinth.

I could, of course, convert the dining parlor into alcoves. It was almost as big as the main parlor, and could be divided into two grand alcoves or four regular ones. But I didn't want to do that. The dining parlor was my formal dining room, and also my conference room for occasions when I needed one, and I didn't want to give it up. Besides, moving my parents' dining table would be a pain, especially if we put it upstairs.

Also, I had a feeling Captain Dusenberry wouldn't approve. It had been his study. It was *his* room—the room where he had died.

"You'll have the extra income from Valentine's Day itself," Nat added.

Called back to business, I nodded. Valentine's Day was a Sunday this year, and I had yielded to customers' requests and Kris's advice that we open that day, with a special "romance" package including fresh roses and chocolate truffles for each guest to take home. Even with the higher price of this offer, we had instantly sold out all the seatings for the day, including the dining parlor. Kris had suggested extending the special for the whole week.

I had hesitated only briefly about working on Valentine's. Tony was more pragmatic than sentimental, so I had no personal reason not to work. We could celebrate in the evening. Or on

Monday.

If he even wanted to celebrate Valentine's. If *he* wasn't working.

I took another sip of oolong.

Small thumps and rumbles reached us from the gift shop. Manny was still maneuvering the heavy things. I'd offered to help, but he'd declined. I had a feeling he thought I'd just be in the way.

Giving myself a mental shake, I turned to Nat with a smile. "How are the plans for Paris going?"

"We have too many of them. We need to pick and choose."

I nodded. Paris was on my bucket list, and there were many museums, many tearooms, many historic attractions. Monet's gardens at Giverny! Versailles! Wineries and cheese makers, not to mention fine dining. I could easily fill a month or more.

Would Tony be interested in Paris? We hadn't talked about a honeymoon yet...

I finished my tea, and set down the cup and saucer. Nat gave me a questioning look, one hand poised over the tea cozy. I shook my head. The thumps from the gift shop had ceased. I stood and went through Dahlia.

Manny was adjusting the board on top of the new credenzas. It was solid oak, stained to match them, and it looked great.

"Perfect," I said. "Thank you, Manny."

He grinned. "You're welcome, *hija*. Now I'm gonna steal my wife and get out of here."

"I owe you a dinner, remember."

Manny had refused to accept payment for his help, so I'd offered to treat him and Nat to dinner at a nice Italian restaurant nearby. We hadn't yet set a date. Manny nodded, and wheeled his hand truck out the front door, picking up the brick he'd used to prop it open.

Nat came into the gift shop with the tea things on a tray, which she set on the sales counter. "It looks beautiful, Ellen!"

I nodded. "Thank you for helping. And for lending me Manny."

"Our pleasure." She gave me a hug and a kiss, then reached for the tea tray.

"I'll get that. Go and get Manny settled for his game."

"All right, sweetie. See you tomorrow."

I saw her out and locked the front door behind her. I had the rest of the day to myself.

I carried the tea tray to the kitchen. There was still tea in the pot, so I poured myself another cup and sipped it while I washed the dishes.

Outside, the sun was bright and the air, I knew, was crisply cold. Late January: the holiday tourists had mostly gone home, and the streets were fairly quiet. It should be a relaxing time, before the Valentine's rush, but the need-to-dos were niggling at me, exerting a subtle pressure.

It was my day off, I reminded them. I'd already worked on tearoom business. Whatever else I did would be for me. Preferably something fun.

I finished my tea and washed the cup, then went upstairs. As I reached the upper floor, there was the ghost of Hyacinth: the two chairs, a small table between them, the oriental rug beneath them, and the tapestry screens behind them. I smiled, and sat in one of the chairs just to see what it felt like. The television, now perched on the cupboard, was framed by the oriental screen, with the chandelier above. Much more classy than a stack of cardboard boxes.

I hadn't been sure about the TV. I'd actually enjoyed not having it for most of a year, but the cooking shows were indeed wonderful. I didn't much care for watching the news.

My phone rang. I pulled it out of my pocket, guiltily hoping it wasn't Gina, who would want to talk about wedding plans.

It was Tony. I smiled and answered. "Hi!"

"Hey, babe. Want to go apartment hunting?"

"Sure. Have you had lunch?"

"Not yet."

It was Sunday; restaurants would be busy

with churchgoers.

"I'll fix us something."

"Be right over."

"OK, bye," I said, though I knew he'd already hung up.

I went into my suite and poked through the fridge in my kitchenette. One advantage of moving would be having an actual kitchen. My search yielded eggs, butter, English muffins, and some spinach that was starting to wilt.

Aha! Eggs Florentine. All I needed was a lemon.

Fortunately, there were always lemons in the tearoom. I fetched one from downstairs, and pulled out pots and pans, humming while I braised the spinach and made Hollandaise sauce. When I heard Tony's bike arrive, I slid the eggs into hot water to poach and turned on the toaster oven to brown the muffins, then went downstairs to let him in.

He was scrubbing his feet on the doormat when I opened the door. He looked up with a grin, came inside and pushed the door shut as he swept me into his arms for a kiss. He smelled like winter and leather.

I returned the kiss warmly, then squirmed free and led him upstairs. "I don't want the eggs to overcook."

They were perfect, and I hastily assembled

the muffins and spinach on plates, then slipped an egg on top of each muffin and poured Hollandaise over all.

"Wow," Tony said, as we sat at the café table. "This is fancy!"

"It's what I had," I told him.

"Mm," he replied, mouth already full.

I smiled and cut myself a bite, egg yolk oozing, a streak of darker gold against the Hollandaise. This was one of my favorite dishes, and I savored the silky sauce, tang of lemon, astringent spinach and the crunch of the muffin.

It was not a low-calorie meal. We would make up for it by walking, I told myself.

Besides, we weren't drinking champagne, so it wasn't *completely* decadent.

"You got some new furniture," Tony commented when he'd finished his first muffin. He nodded toward the hall.

"It's from Poppy and Hyacinth. We dismantled them to make the gift shop bigger."

Tony nodded, mouth full again. I had mentioned to him that I was considering the change, but it had been a few days since I'd seen him, and the decision had been made in the meantime.

"How's your case going?" I asked, though I knew it must be going well or he wouldn't be here.

"Wrapped it up yesterday. Just paperwork left."

"Congratulations!"

"Wish they were all this easy. Perp confessed the minute we showed up at his door."

I nodded, trying to remember if Tony had told me anything about the case. Usually he didn't, unless he wanted to ask a question he thought I could answer.

Or unless I had found the body.

I took another bite of Florentine. Not going to think about that, thanks.

When Tony had finished and I had discreetly scraped up as much sauce as I could get off my plate with my fork, we rinsed the dishes and put them in the dishwasher.

"Should we look online for rentals?" I asked.

"I picked up a paper," Tony said.

"I'll get a highlighter."

We settled on the sofa by the front window. Outside, the sky was sharp blue, with a scattering of light clouds. Maybe the sun would warm things up a bit. Melt down the snow.

We perused the classified ads and marked anything that looked remotely interesting, including a couple of places that were more expensive than the monthly rent we had agreed we could afford. Anything more than ten minutes away from the tearoom in morning traffic, we disqualified. Tony could check in to his job from anywhere; I had to be in the tearoom by at least nine. I *could* plan on coming in early, when the kitchen staff arrived, and avoid the rush hour traffic that way, but it would make for long days for me. Twelve hours, basically—seven to seven —not counting commuting time.

Musing on that, I realized I was putting in nine or ten hours most days anyway. I hadn't thought it was that much. Usually I was in the office, fielding administrative tasks from Kris, and struggling to keep up with messages. But if we were short-handed or particularly busy downstairs, I would help out there.

When we had gone through all the listings, we had seven places to look at. I wrote them all down on a single page, and then added three alternatives—places that were a little too far or a little too expensive—to check out if none of the others was suitable.

If we found a place today, Tony could give notice at his apartment before the end of the month, and start moving. I could move at a more leisurely pace, since I lived at the tearoom, and would not be saving any money on rent.

I made a pot of strong coffee and divided it into two travel mugs, adding cream and sugar to mine. Armed with these and my list, we sallied forth into the cold air and climbed into my car.

Kris would have made a map on the computer with all the addresses marked, and printed it out. I hadn't bothered. Tony was good at visualizing the city and at using his phone to find places.

We started with the nearest place, a duplex within walking distance, less than a mile to the west. It was pretty small and looked a bit run down, and horribly expensive, but Tony called the number anyway.

"Rented," he said after a short conversation.

"Drat. What's next?"

Tony checked the list, then his phone. "Turn right at the next intersection."

The next place was a small-ish apartment in an older building. More modest than Tony's place, and almost twice as expensive due to its proximity to downtown. We marked it a "maybe" and drove on, zig-zagging our way across town, westward and southward. The most promising places were all rented. Apparently we should have started at dawn.

Circling back to two "maybes," we called and discovered one had been rented in the meantime, and were allowed to look at the other: a small guest house behind a modest cinder-block house that was probably older than Tony's and my ages combined. The occupant of the front house, a disheveled middle-aged man who smelled of whiskey, let us into the empty guest house and stood in the living room while we looked around.

The kitchen was small—not much bigger than my kitchenette—and the appliances looked ancient. A cockroach scuttled out of sight as I stepped in, and I wondered what it could have found to eat.

The vinyl floor of the tiny bathroom was yellowed and sagged suspiciously in one corner. Maybe there was wood beneath the carpet in the bedroom and living room, but it would take a lot of work to uncover it, if the owner could be persuaded to give permission. I was sure they would not agree to do it themselves.

Saddest of all, the hope I'd had of being able to garden a little was dashed. The back yard of the main house was cluttered with old tires, broken furniture, a set of box springs from which the fabric had rotted away, and other horrors.

Tony and I exchanged a look. I could tell he knew the answer was no. We thanked the whiskey-scented man and left.

The sun was heading for the horizon, and a cold wind had blown in more clouds. We got in the car and I headed for home, wanting to get away from the depressing guest house.

"I guess we'd better start early next time," I said.

"Yeah. You hungry?"

I was tired, mostly, and disappointed, but the question reminded me that we hadn't eaten since brunch. The coffee was long gone.

"Yes."

"Let's get pizza."

"Great idea!"

Tony called in an order to our favorite pizza place, and it was just coming out of the oven when we arrived. A couple of beers and a salad to share picked up my mood a bit.

"So next Sunday we start early," I said. "We can get breakfast after."

"Babe, we're gonna have to start Friday if we want half a chance."

Oh. Yes, of course—he was right. The classifieds would come out on Friday. Housing was tight in Santa Fe, especially in the area we wanted.

"What's your week look like?" he added.

"We're slow, mostly."

"Can you take Friday off?"

"I think so. I'll ask Nat to come in and cover for me."

He nodded, having just taken a big bite of pizza. I did the same. Mushrooms, pepperoni, and green chile. Comfort food.

I took my crumpled list out of my pocket and looked it over. The sad part was, not one of these places had filled me with joy. The best of them had been merely tolerable.

I was spoiled, perhaps, by living in my Victorian house. But I wasn't demanding a palace. I just wanted a place that wasn't depressing. So far, I hadn't seen it.

Well, I had a week to clarify what I was looking for. "Start by dreaming," Nat had told me when the tearoom was just a fantasy. I had done just that, and I had found the Dusenberry house when I hadn't even been looking. The power of dreams was epic.

I turned the list over and got out a pen. Tony watched while I sketched an idea based on one of the (expensive, already rented) places we had seen that had looked all right from outside. It was an older house that had been divided into apartments. Probably not real adobe, but it was stuccoed in Regulation Santa Fe Brown and had a few bits of decorative tile around the entrance. I added more decoration in my fantasy drawing, and put a little garden in place of the dirt driveway. Flowers in pots and a small bed of herbs and vegetables. I drew in a couple of butterflies, and smiled.

"What's that?" Tony asked.

"What I'd like to find," I said, and turned the picture around to show him.

He studied it, then gave me a mildly skeptical glance. "OK."

"What do you want to find in a new home?"

He took a swig of beer. "A place where we won't be tripping over each other."

I hadn't expected that. So space was a priority for him. His apartment was a decent size, though he hadn't really filled it. I wondered if his family had been crowded when he was growing up. Maybe his father's death had forced them to compromise, find a less expensive home that was small.

"There's no place to park, there," he said, pointing to my drawing.

"The parking is elsewhere."

I wasn't going to let him take the air out of my sails. Dreaming was an important step in creating the life one wanted; I knew that was true.

I ate a bite of salad and looked at my sketch. There was a window by the front door; I had not given it much detail. I imagined looking through it into the room beyond. A nice living room, with *vigas* and *latillas* for the ceiling, and a kiva fireplace in one corner. That would be sweet.

"Starting to snow," Tony said.

I looked up toward the real window nearby. Tiny flakes were drifting down, and it was pretty dark. The sun must have set while we were eating.

"That piece is yours." Tony pointed to the

one remaining slice of pizza.

"You want it? I'm kind of full."

He picked it up and dug in. I got out cash for the tip and dropped my credit card on the ticket. Our server swooped it up and brought back my receipt by the time Tony had finished the pizza and I had picked all the goodies out of the re-maining salad. Tony pulled two tens out of his wallet and offered them to me as I stood up to put on my coat.

"That's more than half," I protested.

"I ate more than half of the pizza."

I took the money, not wanting to argue. Tony was touchy about money.

We went out into what was becoming a blizzard. The snow was already sticking, and the cold might soon turn it into ice. I buttoned up my coat, wishing I'd brought a hat, and scurried to my car. I drove gingerly through the storm, mostly wary of other drivers. There were still tourists in town, and they might be unfamiliar with driving on snow. We got a lot of Texans during ski season.

I lost traction only once, going around a corner. Fortunately I had followed my father's teaching, and put two large bags of cat litter in my trunk for the winter. They provided ballast, and if necessary the litter could be scattered under the tires.

Between the snow and fairly heavy traffic for a Sunday evening, it took almost twice as long as usual to get home. I was relieved when I finally turned into the long driveway behind the tea-room.

"Coming in?" I asked.

"Nah, I better not. I should get home before this gets worse."

I nodded. Tony didn't like staying over when I had staff coming in the next morning. Kind of silly, since they now all knew about our engagement, but I didn't protest. I parked and left the engine running for the sake of the heater.

"Can you get Friday off?" I asked.

"Yeah, I've got tons of vacation. Unless something comes up, I'll come by around seven-thirty."

"OK. See you before then, I hope."

He leaned over in the seat for a kiss. "Definitely you will see me before then."

We got out, and I hurried to the shelter of the *portal* while he hopped on his bike and drove off down the snowy driveway. I was digging my keys out of my purse when I heard an odd squeak.

I froze, even though this had not been a particularly threatening squeak. I looked around, confirming there was no other vehicle parked. No homicidal maniacs that I could see.

The squeak came again, except now it was more of a cry. A bird? No, not in a snowstorm. It was a—

"Mew!"

I lowered my gaze and looked along the *portal*. There, huddled beneath the café table, was a small shadow, obscured by swirling snowflakes.

"Mew!"

I stepped toward it and the shadow shrank back. I could see the reflection of the porch light glowing in its eyes. A tiny, black kitten.

2

MOVING SLOWLY, I approached the table and set my purse and keys on top of it, then crouched down. The kitten was shivering, backed into the corner. Cold, or fear, or both.

"Oh, sweetheart! Where's your mama?"

I reached out my hand, offering fingertips for it to smell. The kitten cringed a little, but didn't run.

"Come on, honey. Let me take you inside and warm you up. Are you hungry?"

"Mew."

Slowly I moved my hand closer, until I was able to pick the kitten up. It weighed nothing, and shivered violently. I tucked it inside my coat and carefully stood, retrieving my purse and keys. The kitten squirmed, and I held it with one hand while I unlocked the door.

A few snowflakes blew in with us. I shut the door and locked it again.

"OK, sweetie. Let's go upstairs and get you something to eat."

I kept talking as I climbed the stairs, hoping to reassure the kitten. It was still shivering, and I felt tiny needle pricks digging into my chest.

"Ow. You're sharp!"

I took it into my suite. Now what? I didn't want to put it down, for fear that it would retreat under the furniture and be hard to catch. I needed a little bed for it.

"Mew!"

"Yes, I know. Here, let me wrap you up."

I grabbed a kitchen towel and bundled the little thing up. It was so tiny! It couldn't be more than a few weeks old. Swaddled in the towel, it wasn't able to stick me with its pinpoint claws. It shivered and squirmed a bit, but I hung onto it while I took off my coat.

Food. What could I feed a cat? Did I have any tuna?

"Let's start with milk."

Worried about the shivering, I decided to warm up the milk. Clutching the little bundle to me, I got out a saucepan. Might as well make cocoa, then. I poured in enough milk for a cup and a bit more, and set it on a burner over medium heat.

"Let's find you something for a bed while that warms up."

Still holding the kitten, I crossed the hall to Kris's office and went into the storage room behind her desk, looking for an empty box. I found one that was almost empty, except for a couple of teapot-shaped spoon rests. It was a good size—tall enough that the kitten shouldn't be able to hop out, small enough for a warm nest. I set the spoon rests on top of another box and returned to my suite with my prize.

The milk wasn't hot yet. I sat in a wing chair by the chimney and set the box on the floor, then moved the bundled kitten to my lap and gently unwrapped it.

It was so scrawny. Still shivering a bit. Its fur was damp, and I rubbed it gently with a corner of the towel. The needle claws clamped into my thigh and I drew a sharp breath. At least I was wearing jeans.

"Mew."

The little face looked up at me. Blue-green eyes—yes it was very young. As I rubbed its fur dry, the eyes closed. A moment later I felt a vibration. It was purring.

"Aw, sweetie. Are you a little boy or a little girl?"

I checked. Girl.

"Let's see if that milk is warm."

Holding the kitten in one hand, I went to the kitchenette. The milk was just starting to steam. I put the towel in the box and gently set the kitty down in it. She immediately started to cry.

"Just for a minute! I'll be right back!"

"Mew! Mew!"

I dipped a spoon in the milk and put a drop on my wrist. Not too hot, but definitely warm. I got out a little sauce dish and spooned some milk into it, then lowered the heat a little and returned to my chair.

"Mew!"

"Here you go."

Carefully, I set the milk dish in a corner of the box. The kitten sniffed it, then started lapping at it. I smiled.

Where had she come from? Cats showed up in my garden occasionally, but I hadn't seen one lately. Maybe I should check. This little one had clearly been separated from her mother.

"Mew."

The milk was gone. She looked up at me.

"Mew."

"Want some more?"

I picked up the dish and returned to the kitchenette. The milk was definitely hot now; steam curled up from the pan. I refilled the dish and set it aside to cool while I mixed cocoa for myself.

Occasional "mew"s came from the box. Returning, I gave the kitty her seconds and watched her while I sipped my cocoa.

She was adorable, but I couldn't keep a kitten in the tearoom. I was pretty sure the health department would disapprove, and no doubt some of my customers were allergic to cats. What would I do?

There was the animal shelter, but I didn't want to resort to that. They euthanized animals that weren't adopted, and people were superstitious about black cats, so her chances of being adopted were lower than average. I'd much rather find a home for her myself.

I'd ask around the staff. Surely someone would like a pet? Goths liked black cats—maybe Kris would take her.

"Mew."

She had finished again. I reached down and picked her up, setting her on my lap. She gazed up at me. I stroked her head, and gently rubbed under her chin. She purred.

What a sweetheart.

Her fur was so soft—baby fluff, still. Now that it was dry it had puffed out, and she looked less pathetic. As I stroked her, she curled up in my lap and closed her eyes, thrumming.

I finished my cocoa, savoring it slowly,

including the cocoa powder dregs, a burst of chocolate power. Setting the empty mug on the table beside me, I carefully picked up the kitten and lowered her into the box. She stirred as I laid her on the towel, but didn't wake.

I carried my mug to the kitchenette, did a quick search, and determined that I had no tuna, but I did have a little leftover chicken. All I needed, then, was something for a litter box.

Julio would kill me if I used one of his pans, but I was pretty sure I had saved the aluminum trays from the staff Christmas party. I grabbed my keys and hurried downstairs, where I unearthed the trays from the back of a cupboard in the kitchen. Taking one, I put the rest back and went out to the hall.

Should have brought my coat. Through the lights around the back door I saw the snow swirling in the darkness. Well, it wouldn't take long.

Leaving the tray in the hall, I went out and plunged through the snow to the back of my car. I extracted one bag of kitty litter and hurried back inside, shivering. I stamped my feet on the doormat, shaking snow off my jeans, then locked up, retrieved the pan, and headed upstairs.

Kitty was still asleep, curled up with the tip of her tail over her nose. Adorable.

Where to put a cat tray? There wasn't a good

spot. This suite had not been designed with pets in mind.

The bathroom would have to do. I opened the litter and coughed at the dust as I poured some into the pan and shook it to spread it evenly. I stashed the litter bag under the sink and went back out to the kitchenette.

More cocoa. I was still chilled. I put the milk on to warm, checked on the kitten, then fetched a sweater from my closet and put it on. I was tempted to build a fire downstairs to warm up the chimney, but settled for turning on my space heater.

While I waited for the milk to heat, I got out the chicken, extracted a piece without too much sauce on it, rinsed it, and minced it, and put it back in the fridge. I'd offer the kitty some when she woke up. With a good book and my cocoa, I settled into the chair for a quiet evening with my new friend.

The beach was peaceful and beautiful, waves gently lapping against the pearly sand, pastel colors painting the sunrise sky, and a lone seagull calling. As I walked along the shore I listened to its mournful cry. No—not mournful; urgent. What could be urgent to a seagull?

"Mew!"

I sat up in bed, suddenly remembering I wasn't alone. Took a deep breath and rubbed my eyes.

"Mew! Mew!"

"OK, I'm coming!"

I got up, dragged on my robe, and stepped into my slippers. It was cold. I hurried into the other room, where I'd left the kitty asleep in her box. She was now awake, scrabbling at the side as she tried to climb out, her little body elongated as she stretched, not quite able to reach the top. I picked her up and carried her to the litter box, speaking softly. She didn't seem afraid any more. I set her down and watched her sniff around.

Please let her know how to use a litter box.

After a moment, she started scratching at the litter. Silently thankful, I left her to do her business and went to get out the chicken.

Glancing out the window, I saw that the snow had continued, leaving a good three or four inches of fresh accumulation on the ground. Good thing I'd brought the kitty in. She would have been in deep trouble if I hadn't.

I put the kettle on and popped a couple of frozen scones into the toaster oven, then put a heaping teaspoon of the minced chicken into the little sauce dish.

"Mew!"

She was at my feet, gazing up at me. I smiled. "Smell good?"

"Mew! Mew! Mew!"

I put her into her box and put the chicken in the corner. She dug in immediately. I watched for a minute, then got out a pen and a notepad and started a list.

Cat food. Litter box scooper.

The kettle boiled and I made tea, then hurried to dress while it steeped. When I came back the scones were done and the kitty's dish was empty.

"Mew!"

"More?"

I gave her half again as much chicken, and added a custard dish full of water to her box. It was getting slightly crowded.

The timer went off, and I took the infuser out of the teapot. Scones would be done in a minute. I poured myself a cup and sipped it. Wandered over to the box to watch the kitten gobbling her food.

What happened to her mother, I wondered? Had this little one gotten lost? Or been dumped? Oh, dear—could there be more? I'd better look around the street for a box.

I hated that humans could be so cruel as to dump baby animals. If you had pets, you were responsible for their welfare, and that included caring for their offspring.

But humans sometimes did the wrong thing. Heck, I sometimes did the wrong thing.

"Mew!"

She had finished her food and was stretching again, trying to get out of the box. As she reached for me, she set one little black hindpaw squarely in the water dish.

"Oh, dear. That won't do."

I put down my tea, then lifted the kitten and the water bowl out of the box. The water I put under the table where I wouldn't kick it by accident. I grabbed the towel and dried her paw. She purred, loudly.

"You are such a cutie!"

I scratched her head and she closed her eyes, blissful. The timer for the scones went off. With the kitten cupped in one hand, I retrieved them and put them on a plate, then got out the butter and cut a couple of pats. The kitten perked up, stretching to sniff.

"You like that, eh?"

I cut a little corner of butter and took it to the box, where I put it in her dish. She squirmed to get at it. I put her down, arranging the towel in a loose nest, and retrieved my scones. The kitten inhaled the butter, then decided it was time to wash her face. Settling into my chair again, I sipped tea and ate my breakfast.

This was going to be a challenging day. I'd

have to keep her in the box, but she'd need the litter box, so I'd have to leave her out at least part of the time. I wished, not for the first time, that my office had a door. I couldn't let her run around loose. A cat in the tearoom would not be good.

So she'd have to stay in my suite, or maybe I could bring the box into my office for a while. I didn't want to leave her alone for a long time, not after she'd been abandoned. Or lost. Maybe Kris would take a shine to her—that would help.

I cleaned up my dishes, preparing for work. The kitten was turning circles in the box. I took her out and set her near the litter box, but she showed no interest.

"All right, my dear. We're going to work."

I collected my phone and keys, and carried the box across the hall to my office. Kris had not yet arrived, so I fired up the samovar, then went back to my suite for the shopping list.

Cat toy, I wrote. Something to keep her amused.

A delicious smell had begun to waft up the stairwell. Not scones; those got baked right before serving, and we weren't open today. But something luscious was going on in the kitchen downstairs.

Pear, I realized. The pear galettes on the January menu. That was it.

I had put the kitten's box close by my desk so I could keep an eye on her. She had settled in for a nap, I was grateful to see. Smiling, I started on my paperwork.

Half an hour later, I heard Kris coming up the stairs. I had caught up on my messages by then, a feat of which I was quite proud. Kris paused, hanging up her coat on the rack outside, then poked her head in my office. She had on black pants (cold day), ankle-high boots, and a thigh-length black tunic, with a long string of jet beads looped into a knot.

"Morning."

"Good morning!" I smiled. "How was your weekend?"

She looked mildly surprised. "All right. Worked on my taxes. Is that box in your way?"

"No, come and look."

The sound of Kris's boots on the wood floor woke the kitten, who looked up as Kris peered into the box.

"Where'd you get that?"

"I found her sheltering on the back portal when I got home from dinner last night."

"You can't have a cat in the tearoom."

"I know. But isn't she cute?"

Right on cue, the kitty yawned adorably and said, "Mew."

"Hm. Is that the ad contract for Valentine's?"

Kris picked up a page from my out box.

"Yes, all signed and done."

"Great. Thanks."

She carried it off to her office without another glance at the kitty. Not promising for a Goth alliance.

"Mew."

I reached down to scritch kitty's head. She batted playfully at my hand, politely keeping in her claws. This reminded me that I needed something to trim those claws. I added it to the list.

"Mew!"

She was stretching again, asking for attention. I picked her up and set her on my lap. She promptly hopped down to the floor.

"Oh, no you don't." I caught her and held her up to eye level. "No running around."

"Mew."

I couldn't just keep her in the box all day, though. What if she needed the litter box?

I got up, collected the teapot that lived on top of the samovar, and went to my suite to make a pot of Lapsang Souchong for Kris. Closing the door, I set the kitten on the floor where I could keep an eye on her. She sniffed around the floorboards, tried unsuccessfully to squeeze herself through the gap under the door, and finally wandered off toward the bathroom. A minute later I heard her scratching in the litter box.

Good. One less thing to worry about.

I went to my dresser and poked around in my jewelry drawer, looking for something for the kitty to play with. I found a length of red ribbon that I rarely wore, stuffed it in my pocket, then hurried back out as the tea timer went off.

No sign of the kitten.

"Where are you, honey?"

I pulled the infuser out of the pot and set it aside, then looked into the bathroom. The kitten was halfway up my jacquard shower curtain.

"Aah! No!"

I detached her, glancing at the curtain for damage. Luckily, I didn't see any.

"No climbing the curtains!" I told her.

"Mew."

I pushed the curtain into the tub, which she wouldn't be able to climb. Kitten in one hand, I carried the teapot to the samovar and set it on top to keep warm, then went back and closed the door to my suite. I would have to take steps to secure all the curtains.

I put kitty back in her box, where she sat looking dejected, mewing. Time for distraction; I produced the ribbon and dangled it over her. She looked at it, then gave it a tentative bat. I raised it just out of reach, teasing. She jumped for it, and proceeded to swat at it with gusto for several minutes, after which, apparently exhausted, she curled up for a nap.

Well and good, but I couldn't do that all day. I didn't want to shut her in my suite all by herself, either. Really, it would be best if I found her a home. If Kris didn't want her, then I'd ask my staff.

Tomorrow. None of the servers came in on Mondays. I'd just have to get through today. I got up and took my teacup to the samovar. Lapsang Souchong was pretty strong, but that was all right for today. I added sugar. I was out of cherry jam, alas.

I looked in on Kris. "Tea?"

"Sure, thanks."

She was intent on her computer, so I fetched a teacup and poured for her, leaving the cup at her elbow. Returning to my desk, I glanced at the kitty. Still sleeping.

I was able to work for a quarter of an hour, until Julio came up from the kitchen with his order list for the week. His chef's cap and pants ensemble today was blue with snowflakes. I hadn't seen that set before. I wondered how big his closet was.

"Can we put the produce order in right away?" he asked. "We're low on fruit."

"Sure," I said. "I'll call Manny."

Produce was cheaper from big distributors,

but I was loyal to Manny for several reasons, not the least of which being that I thought his produce was better quality, on average. I held out my hand for Julio's list, then glanced at the box. Disturbed by our voices, the kitten was awake, blinking and yawning.

"Whatcha got there?" Julio asked.

"A refugee."

I explained the kitten's appearance during the storm. Julio knelt down and picked her up.

"You're a cute one!" He tickled her tummy, to which she instantly and loudly objected.

Julio looked at me. "You'll have to make sure she can't get downstairs."

"I know, but I didn't want to leave her in my suite."

"Take her to the shelter," Kris said from the doorway.

I shook my head. "They euthanize."

"Then get a crate."

That was an idea. I wrote it down on my shopping list. A crate would allow her more room to run around a bit. I could even put a litter pan inside, if I had to leave her for a while. I wondered if crates were expensive.

"You going to keep her?" Julio asked.

"I wasn't planning to. I'm hoping to find her a home."

He scritched her head, then gently put her

back in the box. "Good luck!"

Kris stepped forward. "I'll call in the staples," she said, holding out her hand toward Julio. He stood and gave her his other order list, then headed downstairs. I checked the clock: just past ten. The pet store would be open.

"Kris, could you watch her while I go out to get that crate?"

Kris pressed her lips together. "Make it quick."

"I will. I'll give her a little food, too—then she might sleep."

Maybe. One could hope.

I went to my suite to get the food, and remembered to pick up the water dish. I rinsed it and filled it fresh. Not safe to leave it in the box with the kitty, but I'd offer it to her before I left.

She smelled the food and started crying for it as soon as I returned to the office. I set the dish of chicken down beside her and watched while she ate it. When it was gone I switched the food dish for the water dish. She sniffed it, lapped a couple of times, then turned away.

OK, then.

I removed the water dish and carried the box into Kris's office. "Where shall I put it?"

Kris indicated a spot by the printer. I set the box down and proffered the red ribbon.

"What's that?" Kris said.

"A cat toy. If she cries, you can dangle this to distract her."

Kris took it and dropped it on a corner of her desk, not quite hiding a grimace. "Hurry back."

"I will. Thanks, Kris. Bye, kitty!"

I couldn't help reaching into the box to scritch her a little. She mewed. I left before I could get caught up playing with her.

Such a cutie!

I went back to my office to fetch my list, then remembered Julio's fruit order. I quickly called it in to Manny, aware of the kitten's mewing from Kris's office. After hanging up, I crossed to my suite to collect purse, coat, and scarf. My meager breakfast was telling on me; I grabbed a handful of mixed nuts from the bowl I kept on the counter and munched as I went downstairs.

I looked in on the kitchen on my way out. Hanh glanced up at me from making scones, then returned to her work. Julio was taking a tray of galettes out of the oven.

"I called in the order," I said to him. "Manny says tomorrow morning is the earliest he can bring it."

"That's fine," Julio said, carefully setting the tray on a work table.

"Those smell fantastic," I added.

He gave me a sidelong grin. "Want one?"

"Yes, please."

He grabbed a small plate and slid a galette onto it. "Careful, hot."

"Thank you! I'll be back in a bit."

I carried my prize out into the cold morning, where it gave off steam. The sky was a mixture of sunlight and big, gray clouds—semi-threatening, and also gorgeous. I'd forgotten to put on boots, and the snow tipped into my loafers as I hurried to my car. I set the plate on the dashboard before climbing in. It commenced steaming up my windshield.

Glorious.

I started the engine to warm up the heater, then took a cautious bite of the galette. The glazed pear filling was hot—I almost burned my tongue—and tasted divine. There must be a little hint of alcohol in there, or some spice I couldn't pin down. I'd have to ask Julio.

By the time I had nibbled my way through the pastry, the heater was warming my chilled feet. I set the empty plate on the passenger seat and drove to the nearest pet store.

Crates, I discovered, were prohibitively expensive. I settled for a kitty playpen, sort of like a little tent, big enough for a small litter tray and some space to move around. A helpful clerk recommended a toy that consisted of a little ball trapped in a plastic ring. I also picked out a feather wand, with sparkly bits, that would probably be better than the ribbon for cat-teasing.

I added wet food and kibble and treats to my cart. A combination food and water dish. A little trimmer for her claws. A scoop for the litter box, a small litter box to fit in the playpen, and a replacement bag of litter for my trunk.

I paused before the kitty beds, but decided the towel would do for now. A carrier, though, would be handy for transporting her.

Or I could just use the box.

Don't get carried away, Ellen.

Whoever would be taking her to the vet would need a carrier. If I was fortunate, that wouldn't be me.

I hurried away from all the cute toys and gizmos, and headed to the register to check out. The total made me wince; it was a big investment for an animal I hoped to give away. But these things were necessary to care for her until I found her a home. I would happily donate them to her future owner. I drove back to the tearoom, aware that shopping had taken longer than I'd expected. Leaving the litter in the trunk, I carried the rest upstairs.

Kris was dangling the ribbon over the box as I came into the office. She looked up at me.

"Thank God you're back. She cried the whole time."

I put my purchases on my credenza and hurried into Kris's office to collect the kitten's box. Kitty—who had not cried that I'd heard as I was approaching—greeted me with a chirpy mew.

"Thank you for watching her," I said, picking up the box. "I hope she wasn't too distracting."

Kris made a non-committal noise and turned to her computer. I carried the box into my office.

"Wait 'til you see what I've brought you!" I told the kitten.

I got out the playpen and started setting it up. The kitten mewed before I had figured it out, so I gave her a couple of treats to keep her busy. I put the playpen near my desk, under the slope of the roof, and put the ring toy inside it. I needed litter for the small tray.

"OK, kitty, come check this out!"

I lifted her out of the box, grabbed the towel as well, and put them both into the pen, then zipped the mesh top shut. The kitten stood looking around, then began to sniff the bottom edge of the playpen. I went to my suite to fill the litter tray, taking the box along with me. When I returned, the kitten was sniffing at the ring toy. She looked up at me.

"Pretty cool, eh?" I said, unzipping the top so I could put the litter tray in.

She looked a little forlorn, maybe because of

all the new things, so I picked her up and cuddled her, stroking her. "You're going to like this better, I promise."

She butted her little black head against my hand. I scritched between her ears, and she started to thrum. I carried her to my desk and held her while I checked my email and messages. Nothing urgent. I looked at my phone, and saw that I'd missed a text from Gina, suggesting we meet for lunch. It was after twelve, so I texted back an apology for missing the chance.

The kitten began to squirm. I took her back to the playpen and set her down in the middle. She had three choices: litter box, toy, or bed. She looked up at me.

"Mew."

Ah. Maybe a fourth choice was needed.

Remembering her climbing adventure with the curtains, I zipped the pen shut, then found the new food dish and carried it to my suite to wash it. I picked up a spoon and filled a measuring cup with water (easier to pour than to carry a bowl of water across the hall), and returned to my office.

Opening a can of kitten food, I put it in one side of the food dish, then set it in the pen beside the kitten. By the time I fetched the water from my credenza, kitty was sitting in the empty side of the dish, happily gobbling the food. I put the measuring cup down and zipped the pen shut. That should keep her busy for a little while.

Come to think of it, lunch sounded like a good idea. I went back to my suite and warmed up the rest of the leftover chicken, then sat by the front window in the hall to eat, watching the sky. The dark clouds hung heavy; could mean more snow. I remembered my intention to look for a box, in case the kitty had been part of an abandoned litter. When I was finished with lunch I looked in on her and saw she was sleeping. I fetched my coat and went downstairs.

The air outside was not much warmer than it had been earlier. I pulled on my gloves and walked down the driveway, then up the length of the street, peering under bushes and checking behind trees. I found no box, heard no plaintive cries. Relieved, I headed back to the house, looking forward to a hot cuppa.

Just before I reached the driveway, Nat's car came up the street. I waved as she turned in. In all the fuss over the kitten, I'd forgotten that my aunt was coming in today to help me stock the new shelves in the gift shop. I lengthened my stride in the wake of her car, and arrived as she was getting out. She had on a coat she'd bought from a local weaver years ago—gray, white, and black—beautiful work, and it still looked new. A red scarf provided a splash of color.

Nat greeted me with a smile and a hug. "Anything left for me to do?"

"Well, um... yes. I've been a bit distracted, actually. I haven't started."

"Oh! Then we'd better get going!"

We headed inside. "Yes. I want tea, though. I'll make it."

"Sleep late?" she said, giving me a sidelong smile.

"No. In fact—well, come up with me and you'll see."

Nat hung her coat in the hall and followed me up the stairs to my office. She paused in the doorway, taking in the playpen and the jumble on my credenza. Self-conscious, I picked up an empty pet store bag and folded it. Usually I kept my office tidy. "You got a puppy?" Nat said.

"A kitten. She was on the back *portal* when I got home last night, sheltering from the snow."

Nat peered through the top of the playpen. "Oh! She's so tiny!"

Hearing our voices, the kitten looked up, blinking, and yawned. Nat crouched down for a closer look.

"Want to hold her? We can take her out."

"Maybe later. We've got work to do."

Since we were upstairs, I went into Kris's office and stepped past her desk to the storage room. Kris was on the phone, but she gave Nat a smile and a wave. I brought out two boxes of inventory, handed them to Nat, and went back for two more. That would get us started.

Downstairs, we could hear salsa music faintly from the kitchen. I paused to put a kettle on in the butler's pantry, then we went into the gift shop, where the new, empty shelves and island looked rather huge.

I made tea while Nat got out price tags and a box cutter, then we got to work. Opening the boxes felt a little like Christmas. I knew from the sender's name that one of them contained bulk tea that we'd have to break down and package for sale, but the others were surprises: decorative teaspoons, strainers, and infusers; tea cozies in cheerful fabrics; and valentine cards.

I glanced toward our small display of greeting cards. "I guess we should go ahead and put these out."

"Yes, do," Nat said, putting price tags on spoons. "It's less than a week until February."

Was it? Yikes!

I tagged the cards, then took them over to the display. To make room for them I took out a few leftover holiday cards and a couple of others that had been around a while. The valentines made a splash of pink and red in the display, like a bouquet of roses. There was one I particularly liked, with a photo of a couple dancing in the rain, the woman in a red dress, the man in a dashing suit. On impulse, I took it out and marked it down in my log of inventory removed for personal use. I needed a card to give Tony.

Gradually, the new space filled up with pretty things. I moved a display of teacups into one of the new china cupboards, and expanded the packaged tea to fill the whole set of shelves it had formerly shared. The tea cozies went by the teapots.

Each time I went upstairs for another box, I checked on the kitten. As I fetched out a box of lace doilies and napkins, I heard a rattling sound. It was the ring toy; the ball rattled as the kitten batted it around and around the ring. I hope the noise wasn't bothering Kris.

By four o'clock, the displays were all filled and I was famished. Lunch had been a little light, and I'd made quite a few trips up the stairs.

"Want some tea?" I asked Nat, who was tidying up the empty boxes, breaking them down for recycling.

"Absolutely!"

"Scones?"

"Just one."

"I'll get them going upstairs. Come on up when you're through here."

Julio and Hanh had gone home a couple of hours earlier. I resisted the temptation to steal a couple of the pear galettes. Instead, I snagged a ripe pear and sliced it up while the scones were baking in my toaster oven. Taking the timer with me, I crossed the hall to look in on the kitten.

"Mew!" she called as I came in, pressing her face against the screen window of the playpen.

I couldn't resist playing with her a little. I took her out, then put a handful of kibble in the food dish and some water in the other side. She purred loudly. A brief cuddle, then the timer went off and I put her back.

Kris came out of her office and took her coat down from the rack. "I'm off. See you tomorrow."

"Want to stay for a cuppa?"

"No, thanks. I have errands."

"OK. Have a good evening."

I rescued the scones, and while they were cooling I made tea and assembled a tray. I had just carried it out to the sitting area when Nat came up. She settled into a chair and accepted a cup of Darjeeling.

"Thank you, dear."

"Thank *you,* for helping with the shop. It would have taken me forever alone."

"It looks great. I kept wanting to browse."
I chuckled, then sipped my own tea and sighed. A few snowflakes drifted and swirled outside the window.

"Well, your idea of putting all the Valentine's things on the new island was brilliant," I said. "We may keep that a seasonal display."

"It would make it easy to change out the merchandise." Nat took a slice of pear from the plate. "Mmm."

I followed suit. "So good. Manny brings us the best fruit."

"You're a star customer. He's always bragging on you, passing out tearoom cards."

"You found a good one."

She smiled. "So did you."

We watched the snow dancing, quietly comfortable together. The pear and the scones duly vanished. One last cuppa, then Nat rose.

"I'd better get home and make dinner."

"Thanks again."

"Need me tomorrow?"

"I don't think so. Not until Thursday. Let me know when I can take you and Manny to dinner."

"Right. See you Thursday, then."

I stood. "Want to say goodbye to the kitten?"

"Goodbye, kitten," Nat said, pausing in the office doorway. She looked at me. "I hope you find her a good home. You really can't keep her here."

"I know."

Stifling a sigh, I went downstairs with Nat,

helped her into her beautiful woven coat, then returned to clear the tea things. The snow was falling more heavily now.

So far, no one had fallen completely in love with my little black friend. I would let the servers know about her tomorrow and hope that one of them would take her. Otherwise, I'd have to place an ad.

Maybe Gina would like her? She had a big, loving, Italian heart. But she didn't have any pets. In fact, I couldn't remember her ever having pets. Hmmm.

In case she had answered my text, I fetched my phone and checked for messages. Gina had indeed responded, with "Tomorrow?"

I checked my calendar to make sure I had no other obligations, and sent back a confirmation. She wanted to talk about the wedding, I knew. But maybe she'd spare some love for a little black kitten.

I was on the Santa Fe Plaza, wearing a long white dress and gold locket and chain. I had a lace parasol and was listening to a brass band playing in the gazebo. Other people were standing around, or sitting on picnic blankets, enjoying the music. A scruffy dog wandered by, looking for handouts from the picnickers.

A man I didn't recognize—Hispanic, with a mustache—sauntered up, brandishing a Colt Navy pistol. Bullets fell out of his pockets, scattering on the ground. I was angry about the mess he was making. Couldn't he tell people were trying to enjoy a concert?

I glared at him, and he grinned back at me, still waving his gun. The music got louder, more strident, and repetitive, as though it was stuck, playing one note over and over...

My alarm.

Groggy, I swatted at the clock and managed to hit the snooze button.

What was *that* all about?

I got up and checked on the kitten. Still asleep in her box.

I thought about the dream as I showered and dressed. Probably it was my subconscious reminding me about my research plans. Or maybe Captain Dusenberry was giving me a nudge in my dreams? Could ghosts do that?

When I emerged from the shower I heard the kitten crying. I picked her up out of the box and set her on the floor. She made a beeline for the litter box in the bathroom. While she was busy, I opened a can of wet food for her breakfast, putting it in the double dish that I'd brought over the night before. The smell of the food brought her running back—a little black fluff ball skittering across the floor. I couldn't help but smile.

An hour later I was back in my office, fed and dressed and ready to promote my protégée. I had tidied away all the packaging, stashed the extra food in my pantry cupboard, and set the sparkly feather wand close at hand near the playpen.

The kitten was attacking the ring toy with gusto, chasing the ball back and forth. We were ready for the servers to arrive and fall in love with her.

Until then, I would catch up on my messages and then pursue my investigations regarding Captain Dusenberry's death. Feeling virtuous, I glanced through the mercifully small stack of message slips from the previous afternoon, fired off two texts and one call to deal with them, then opened my Dusenberry file.

I had two documents from Sonja at the Archives still waiting to be read: Manuel Hidalgo's diary and Seraphina Ruiz's letters. Perusing them would probably take more time than I should spend during a work day. Most of the rest of the list was questions I needed to ask.

I sent Sonja an email requesting Captain Dusenberry's official correspondence and quartermaster records for the month before his death. I hoped to find some mention in them of his setting up someone to fill in for him while he was away (eloping).

Next, I found Mr. Quentin's card in my file from the ghost tours last fall, and called him to ask whether he had a metal detector or knew someone who did. I got his voicemail, so I left my query in a brief message.

That left three questions I needed to ask Eduardo Hidalgo, plus the task of photographing Maria's letters to the captain, which I'd forgotten to do before taking them to the bank. The latter would require some time and effort, so I postponed it for now and pondered how best to approach Mr. Hidalgo.

Should I invite him to tea? Drop by his office again? Take some scones?

I had no idea whether he'd enjoy afternoon tea, but few men would turn down fresh baked goods. I could take scones plus maybe a couple of the pear galettes, if I could wheedle them out of Julio. Probably best to set up a time, rather than just drop by. I unearthed Mr. Hidalgo's card and called.

Voicemail again. I glanced at the time: 9:15. Possibly too early for an elderly gentleman who managed a plaza that housed shops and restaurants, most of which didn't open before 10:00. I left a polite message asking if I might drop by sometime this week. As I put down the phone, I heard the rumble of a large truck coming up the driveway.

Manny, with Julio's produce order.

I got up to go greet him, pausing to glance in at Kris. "Need anything from downstairs?"

She shook her head. "Is there tea?"

I checked the pot keeping warm on top of the samovar. "Enough for a cup."

"I'll make another pot."

Manny and Julio were moving boxes around and discussing raspberries from Chile. I kept out of the way until they were finished, then caught Manny on his way out.

"Thank you, Tío!"

He caught me in a brisk hug. "No problemo. I heard you have a new pet!"

"Just until I find her a home. Want to meet her? She's upstairs."

"Not today. Got a full schedule."

"OK. Thanks again!"

Manny grabbed his hand truck, paused at the door as Mick and Dee came in, then departed with a cheery wave. I watched him climb into his truck, noted that the driveway was pretty slushy, and wondered if I'd need to add more gravel this year.

Closing the door, I followed Dee into the little hall outside the butler's pantry. As she stashed her purse in a locker, hung up her coat, and donned one of our lace-trimmed white aprons over her lavender dress, I struck up a chat.

"How was your weekend?"

"Oh, it was great! I skied all day Saturday, and went to a movie Sunday."

"That sounds fun. Did Mick go with you?"

A tinge of color darkened her cheeks, accompanied by a shy smile. "No, I had a date."

"Ah," I said, smiling back.

"How about you?" she asked, freeing her long, pale hair from the back of the apron.

"Well, we made some changes in the gift shop over the weekend. Come and see when you have a minute."

"I will, as soon as I make some tea."

Completely sympathetic to that motive, I left her to fire up the big urn in the butler's pantry and strolled down the hall to the shop to make sure everything was in order. Looking in from the doorway, it was still a bit of a shock to see that Poppy and Hyacinth were gone.

The first thing that caught my eye was the red and pink splash of Valentine's merchandise on the new island. I walked to it, admiring the display and thinking about the flow of the new arrangement

From here, the next thing I noticed was the china cabinets against the wall—two new ones flanking the fireplace, and then the existing ones along the south wall, filled with teacups, teapots, sugar and creamer sets, and dessert plates. Continuing along that wall I came to the tea display, now an entire cabinet of its own. We had added glass jars of three "featured" teas for the month, so that people could see the leaves, and other ingredients where there were any. Rose petals were especially pretty.

The second island held an array of linens and accessories, plus little gift items and knick-knacks. Looking toward the rest of the shop from there, one could browse the greeting cards, look through a small selection of tea-related books, choose a cozy or a decorative tea caddy—perhaps those should go over with the tea—and, finally, be tempted by fresh scones and sweets in the small display case by the sales counter.

It seemed a good flow. We would see how it worked out. To make up for the loss of Poppy and Hyacinth, we needed to increase gift shop sales by at least eight percent. Kris had assured me we would.

Dee joined me, and let out a little crow of delight. "This is great! No more edging through Poppy with a tray for Dahlia or Violet. Yay!"

"Yes, it should make things less awkward."

"I always felt so bad, interrupting them, especially if they were hungry and had to watch the food go by. Wow, I love all the Valentines stuff!"

Dee picked up a black mug with electric red hearts all over it, an item about which I had been dubious.

We all have different tastes, I reminded myself.

I wanted to get her upstairs. Unable to think of a more subtle ploy, I announced, "I'd better go up and check on the kitten."

"You've got a kitten?" Dee said, eyes widening.

"She turned up on the *portal* Sunday night, sheltering from the snowstorm."

"Oh, I love baby animals! Can I see her?"

"Sure, come on up."

Dee followed me upstairs, and let out a little squeal of delight when we entered my office. The kitten looked up, startled, crouched as if to flee.

"Oh, what a darling! Hi, kitty!"

I opened the playpen roof, picked up the kitten, and deposited her into Dee's hands. Dee cooed and stroked her. The kitten, after a moment, began to purr.

"Oh, she's adorable! What's her name?"

"I haven't named her."

"Aren't you going to keep her?"

"I really can't keep a cat in the tearoom. She

needs space to run around."

"You should name her Minuit!"

I liked that. Midnight, with a dash of minuet. Very French.

"You could name her that," I said. "Would you like to adopt her?"

"Oh, I'd love to!" Dee nuzzled the little fluff ball. "But my apartment building doesn't allow pets."

Damn.

Hiding my disappointment, I watched Dee play with the kitten for a couple more minutes. She put her back in the pen, then picked up the feather wand and wiggled it over the kitten's head. The kitten froze, uncertain, then reached up a tentative paw. Dee pulled the toy just out of reach, and the kitten jumped up at it.

I decided I needed tea. Leaving Dee to her fun, I fetched my cup, then went to the samovar.

Kris had been true to her word; a fresh pot of Keemun sat on top. I filled my cup and stood in the doorway of my office, watching Dee. Her reaction to the kitten was all I could have wished, but it was unrealistic to expect she might move just to adopt a pet.

"Ellen, Eduardo Hidalgo is on hold for you," Kris called from her desk. "Do you want to take it?"

I stepped into her office. "Yes, thanks."

As I headed for my desk, Dee got to her feet and set the feather wand aside, then gave the kitten a last scritch before closing the playpen. She tiptoed out, flashing me a big smile as I picked up the phone.

"Mr. Hidalgo, thanks for returning my call."

"Always nice to hear from a pretty lady. What can I do for you?"

"I'd like to talk to you about Tía Maria and other members of your family for half an hour or so. Is there a time this week when it would be convenient for me to visit? Or if you'd like, you could come to my tearoom and I'll serve you tea and lunch."

"That is too tempting. I'd better just meet you here," he said. "How about Thursday morning?"

"That works. What time?"

"Ten-thirty would be good."

"Ten-thirty it is. Thank you!"

I added the date to my calendar. I'd ask Julio to make up some extra pear galettes.

Maybe I should tell Mr. Hidalgo about Maria's letters. Or even...

I glanced at the week on my calendar. Friday morning was apartment-hunting, and today I had lunch with Gina, but it was otherwise clear until Thursday. If I could get by the bank and pick up the letters, and take photos, then I could print out copies for Mr. Hidalgo.

That felt good. I hadn't shared the letters with many people, but this would give me something to offer Mr. Hidalgo in exchange for the information I was asking from him. I'd have to be careful to take good pictures.

Or...

I knew a professional photographer. Smiling, I got up, looked in on the kitten who was napping after the excitement of Dee's visit, and went downstairs to talk to Julio.

He and Hanh were both bustling. Large trays sat on the work counter, and Julio was at the big stand mixer, while Hanh sliced heaps of mushrooms. Those were for the mushroom turnovers, a fabulous savory. Now I wanted one.

I would have to invite someone to tea this week, that was all. Too bad Mr. Hidalgo had declined.

I met Hanh's inquiring glance with a nod and a smile. She nodded back and kept working. I strolled over to Julio, who turned off the rather noisy mixer.

"Thank you," I said. "Is Owen terribly busy this week? I have a photography job if he's interested. I thought I'd check with you before calling."

"Well, I'm not positive, but I think he'd probably have time."

"OK, thanks. I'll give him a call."

"Is it for an ad? Will you need food?"

"No—this is something else. A personal project."

Julio's brows rose, but he made no comment. Instead he turned the mixer back on, an effective dismissal. I left, escaping the noise, and looked in on the gift shop before going back up.

Dee and Rosa were both there, admiring the new layout and browsing the merchandise. That was fine with me; I encouraged the staff to be familiar with our offerings.

Rosa looked up from the Valentine's display. "Dee says you have a kitty!"

"Yes. Feel free to come up and meet her on your break."

I glanced at the clock—less than an hour until we opened. Leaving the servers to organize for our first customers, I headed up to my office. Back to the business cards, this time for Owen Hughes. He answered on the third ring.

"Hi, Owen, it's Ellen Rosings. I hope I'm not calling too early."

"Enchanté. Not at all."

"I have a photography project I was wondering if you might help me with. Not very artistic, I'm afraid. It's documentation."

"Of?"

"Some historic letters."

"From Captain Dusenberry?"

"Well, they belonged to him. They were written to him."

"Sounds fascinating. I'd be happy to help."

"Oh, good! Thank you."

We discussed timing and settled on that afternoon. Wednesday was Julio's day off, so he and Owen might have plans, and Thursday was when I would visit Mr. Hidalgo, hopefully with printouts of the letters in hand. I apologized to Owen for the short notice, but he brushed it off with some charming words about being at my service any time.

I would not call Owen old-fashioned, but he certainly had a classic way of flirting. It might have bothered me, except that I knew Julio was aware of it. I figured it was just Owen's way.

Besides, it was nice to have one's hand kissed now and then.

I put his card away and grabbed my cell phone. I had just enough time to go to the bank and get the letters before meeting Gina for lunch. I put some kibble in the kitten's bowl and made sure she had water, then stepped into Kris's office.

"I've got an errand and then a lunch date. Could you look in on the kitten now and then?"

"OK."

"Thanks. Anything to go to the bank?"

Kris shook her head.

"See you this afternoon, then. Owen's coming at two to take some photos for me."

I mentioned that in case lunch with Gina ran later than I expected, and Owen showed up before me. I planned to be back before two, but one never knew.

I fetched my coat and purse from my suite, making sure I had the key to my safety deposit box. Locking the door, I headed for the stairs.

"Mew."

I looked into my office. The kitty stretched up toward the roof of the playpen. She couldn't reach it, and leaned against the screen wall instead, her little forepaws outstretched.

"Minuit? Is that your name?" I asked, rubbing a finger on the screen in front of her nose. She sniffed it, then sat down and peered at me. I straightened. "I'll be back, sweetie."

The last thing I heard as I headed down the stairs was the rattle of the ball in the ring toy.

3

THE BANK WASN'T BUSY, FORTUNATELY. I collected the letters, stashed them in my glove box, and got to Gina's favorite bistro five minutes early. A waiter led me to her table by the window—Gina was a regular here, for business lunches—and brought me coffee. The day was clear and cold. I looked out at the bright blue sky and mused about Captain Dusenberry's elopement plans.

Gina's arrival was preceded by her voice cheerily exchanging greetings with the host at the door. She appeared in her red wool coat over a stylish burgundy dress, coming to the table with open arms. I stood for a hug.

"It feels like forever," she said. "How was Ghost Ranch?"

"Oh, it was fun. Mostly fun."

A delighted smile crinkled the corners of her

eyes. "Don't tell me. You found a body."

I gave her a repressive glance as I resumed my seat. She let out a gusty laugh.

"You did! Tell me all about it."

I entertained her with a brief summary of my long weekend retreat with Tony and the unfortunate increase of my tally of finding dead bodies. She laughed at all the right places, which soothed my ruffled feathers. I disliked being a corpse magnet, but I was becoming resigned to it. Perhaps it was my mission in life to find the dead, so that their sad stories could be resolved. If that was so, then marrying a homicide detective was undoubtedly a good move.

And at least the latest body had not turned up in my tearoom.

The waiter came and took our order, replenished my coffee, and brought Gina a glass of wine. Gina took a swallow, smiled, and then faced me with her "let's do business" look.

"So, about the wedding," she said, opening a petite pocket notebook with a cute little matching pen.

"It's still on," I told her.

She chuckled. "I assume Joe's going to give you away."

"Nat and Manny, actually."

She looked surprised, then nodded. "OK. But Joe will be there."

"As far as I know."

"Maybe Tony could have him as a grooms-man."

"That's up to Tony," I said. I didn't add that it was highly doubtful. My brother had rather offended Tony—not to mention me—over the Christmas holiday, and though we'd worked it out, there was still some tension there. Gina had not been present for that little episode, but she'd gone skiing with Joe and had confessed to me that she'd had a crush on him back when we were all in high school.

Mental note: throw the bridal bouquet out of Gina's reach, if possible.

"All right. So who are your bridesmaids?" Gina asked.

"Um. Tony's sister, Angela."

She made a note, then looked up at me expectantly.

"She's the only one I've asked."

"Well, you'd better start asking. Time's a-wastin'."

"I don't think there's anyone else, actually."

"What about Kris?"

A Goth bridesmaid? Um...

I prided myself on being open-minded, but Kris's mood had been especially prickly lately. The servers were all several years younger than I. I might have asked Vi, if she hadn't been killed.

"I hadn't really planned on having any of my staff in the wedding party." Seeing Gina's disappointment, I added, "It won't be a huge wedding."

"Are you sure there's no one else you want to ask? What about classmates?"

"Honestly, Gina, you're the only one I've stayed in touch with."

I hadn't thought about it, but that was true. College, and my parents' deaths, had caused a social separation for me. I was not who I'd been in high school, and with the exception of Gina, I'd mostly lost touch with that part of my life.

I didn't have any friends. Realizing that was a shock. But I hadn't had time for friends. The tearoom was my life. I had lots of friendly *acquaintances,* but very few close friends—few confidants. My family, and Gina, and Tony. That was it.

I sipped my coffee and considered ordering wine.

"Well, think about it," Gina said. "Go over your Christmas card list. There might be some-one you're overlooking."

"I'll do that."

"Meanwhile, put me in touch with Angela."

"OK. Would you like to have tea, the three of us?"

"That would be fab!"

"Probably a weekend. She's in school."

"Saturday? We can go shopping for dresses—*before* tea, of course."

Oh, God. Dresses. Ay yi yi.

"I'll ask if she's free," I said.

Maybe Angela would like to have the kitten, I mused as I made a note to call her.

"While you're looking at your Christmas list," Gina said, "make me a copy so I can invite people to your shower."

"I don't—"

"Oh, yes you do. You are getting a shower, girl. That's my job, don't you worry about it. Just relax and enjoy it."

The martial look in her eye shut me up. I was going to have to choose my battles, it seemed. A shower would be fun, I told myself. Let Gina have her way. This was partly about letting her shine. Certain other matters were not within the maid of honor's purview, such as the guest list for the wedding. That was mine, and Tony's, and we would keep it small.

"Have you decided where to have the ceremony?" Gina asked.

"Not yet."

"Will it be Catholic? I could check about getting you the cathedral. Nonna's got friends."

"Oh, that's far too big," I said, rather

alarmed. "Thank you, but no. It's going to be fairly small. And it may not be Catholic. I'm not."

"OK. How about Loretto Chapel? It's no longer consecrated, if that worries you."

Loretto Chapel was indeed much smaller, and historic, and charming. I hadn't thought about it, but my initial instinct was to say no.

"I'm thinking about a garden wedding, maybe," I said.

Gina shot me a look. "Not at your place."

"No, no."

"So informal?"

"I...I really need to discuss some of these things with Tony."

Gina gave a nod. "Yes, you do."

"There's still time."

"Some things you have to do far in advance, and booking the venue is one of them," Gina said. "I'd make that your priority, for starters."

"You're right. I'll talk to Tony."

"Find out who his best man will be, and put me in touch."

"OK."

Our lunch arrived, a welcome distraction. I was beginning to feel a bit railroaded. Gina set aside her notebook, smiled, and asked me if I'd chosen my colors. We chatted about that through the meal, and I felt less pressured. Gina had no opinions, except that she thought it might be good to avoid wisteria colors—lavender, light purples. I had been thinking the same thing. This was not a Wisteria Tearoom event. I needed to keep the wedding separate from my work.

"Is Julio making the cake?"

"Maybe. I did ask him to cater, and he said yes."

"Excellent!"

A server came by with a coffee pot. I was already buzzing a bit from caffeine, so I asked for just half a cup and added some cream. As I stirred the clouds, I remembered that it had been a wedding where I'd found Julio. A wedding cake, to be specific.

I should definitely ask him to make mine. It would bring things full circle.

Funny how such patterns were so appealing. On a technical level it shouldn't matter who made my wedding cake, as long as they were competent, but there was more to the situation than that. Asking Julio to make my cake, after finding him from a cake he'd made, would reaffirm my approval of all that he was, and would strengthen our relationship. Something like that might make a difference if he was offered a job somewhere else.

God forbid! I banished the thought. Julio was essential to the tearoom.

"May I bring you ladies some dessert?" The waiter offered a slip of paper bearing dangerous information.

"Sorry, not today," Gina said. "I have a two o'clock."

"So do I," I said.

The waiter bowed and went off to tally up the bill. Gina opened her little notebook.

"So—I need you to send me Angela's contact info, and your colors, the venue when you have it, and whether this Saturday is good for dress-shopping and tea with Angela. Do you want me to make you a list?"

"Um—text me?"

"OK."

She dictated the list into her phone, and a moment later mine silently buzzed in my purse. We paid the bill, hugged, and went our separate ways. Since the bistro wasn't far from Loretto Chapel, I drove past it on my way home. Its Gothic ornamentation and proportions—tall and narrow—had always appealed to me. It was lovely inside as well, all golden stone, and had interesting, echoey acoustics. In December I'd gone to a concert there, to hear Ramon play with an ensemble. I liked the place, but it just didn't feel right for the wedding. All that stone was a little cold.

Flowers. I wanted to be surrounded by

flowers and trees, not stone.

I headed home, arriving a few minutes before two. I hurried to set up the table in the dining parlor. Owen had asked for that room, and for a tablecloth I didn't mind him putting tape on. I fetched out an old cloth that I used for crafting, and moved the floral centerpiece to the sideboard, debating whether to build up the fire. It had been lit that morning and had now fallen to coals. The fireplace still radiated warmth, though—there was a fire on the other side, for the enjoyment of the customers in the main parlor. I decided to leave it be.

I was just folding up the good lace cloth when Owen came in, carrying a large folio and his camera bag. He had on a gray turtleneck and a herringbone jacket, with his long hair held back by a gorgeous sand-cast silver clip.

"Hi, Ellen. You're looking smart today." He smiled.

"Thanks, so are you! And thanks again for coming on short notice," I said. "Would you like some tea?"

"Maybe after. I'm curious to see these letters."

He put down his bag and the folio, then took off the jacket and hung it on a chair. I spread the old tablecloth over the table.

"I'll go fetch them," I said. Owen nodded and

opened his folio.

I had left the letters in the glove box of my car, figuring they'd be as safe there as in my desk. I had to dart upstairs for my keys. When I returned, Owen had transformed the dining table into a mini-photography studio. A big sheet of white poster board was taped to the cloth, and over it a tripod loomed at an angle. Two of the legs were short; the third was long and clipped to the edge of the table, so that the tripod leaned forward toward the poster board. Owen was mounting his camera on this contraption when I came in.

"You've done this before, I see."

He looked up at me with a grin. "A couple of times."

"Do you want the chandelier on?"

"No, I prefer natural light. You could open the curtains, if you don't mind."

They were lace, but they did block some light and the sun was on the other side of the house. I set the letters on the sideboard and went to pull the curtains back. Owen put a sheet of blank paper on the poster board and fiddled with the camera's settings. I returned to the letters, a little nervous about sharing them, and gently eased the ribbon off the packet.

"Do you have gloves?" Owen asked.

"In the kitchen," I said. "Shall I get some?"

"No, I mean cloth gloves. Cotton, preferably. Those look old enough that they shouldn't be handled bare-handed." He nodded toward the letters in my hands.

"Oh! Well, yes, I have some gloves."

"Go get them, if you don't mind."

I took the letters with me, feeling flustered. I should have known that they needed extra protection. But I did know; that was why I had asked Owen to photograph them. Ay, yi, yi. I needed to get them to the museum.

I dug my glove box out of my dresser and opened it, looking for a pair of plain white cotton gloves. My old marching band gloves would have worked, except the fingertips were cut out. I set them aside, along with a pair of eighteen-button gloves that would be a bit excessive for the occasion. Beneath was a pair of short gloves that had been my grandmother's. They were white cotton, with white embroidery on the backs. She would have worn them to church, back in the day.

Good enough. I put them on, stretching the stiff cotton into place between my fingers, before I picked up the letters.

Returning to the dining parlor, I found Owen gazing out the windows. He turned as I came in.

"Sorry I took so long."

"No problem. Let's have the first letter here."

He removed the blank page from the poster board.

I took a napkin out of the sideboard, spread it on top, and laid the letters on it, then picked up the first one and carefully opened it. I gently set it on the poster board.

"Square it up, please. A little to the left."

Owen let me handle the letter, looking through the camera and giving me instructions to adjust the placement of the page. Finally he handed me a ruler and a pencil.

"Mark the board where the bottom edge falls, and at the corners."

"Some of the letters are different sizes," I said.

"That's OK. It's just to give us a guideline."

I did as he asked, then got out of the way. Owen shot several pictures, studying the results on the camera viewer and making adjustments, then finally asked me to turn the page over. I did so, and he shot several more images.

"OK, good. Next letter."

I lined it up on the pencil marks, and carefully refolded the first letter, setting it beside the others as the beginning of a "finished" stack. It took a while to go through all of them, though there was less fiddling with the camera settings as we went on. As I handled the letters, memories of my marginal success at reading the ones that were in Spanish returned, as did my sadness about Maria and the captain's thwarted attempt to marry. I did need to get them translated. There were still mysteries here.

By the time we finished, the light was starting to fade. I gently straightened the stack of letters and eased the ribbon back onto it while Owen disassembled his equipment.

"Thank you so much, Owen. Please send me your bill."

"I will. Do you want me to download these for you right now, or put them on a data stick?"

"Data stick would be fine, if you don't mind dropping it by tomorrow. I need to print out some of the photos for Thursday."

"You've got it. And by the way, congratulations. Julio tells me you're getting married."

"Oh. Yes." I felt the color rising in my cheeks. "I don't suppose you do weddings?"

He smiled, eyes crinkling with amusement. "I wasn't fishing for a gig."

"I didn't think you were. It's just one more thing, and I hadn't thought of it, but we'll need a photographer. Sorry, I'm a little overwhelmed."

"Understandable. To answer your question, I don't usually do weddings, but I'm willing to make an exception for a friend." The smile that accompanied this statement set my heart fluttering a bit.

"Thank you," I said. "I'll let you know. Or, I guess Julio will let you know. He's agreed to cater—he must have told you."

"He did."

Our gazes held for a moment, and I felt a warmth inside. Owen was so kind, usually when I least expected it.

I took a steadying breath. "Would you like that tea now?"

"Another day, I think," Owen said, smiling. "It's getting late."

He was right. My awareness of the tearoom's activity in the background told me the business day was ending. The main parlor, directly west of us, had fallen quiet. Earlier there had been a murmur of conversations; now there was silence except for the occasional clink of a dish as the servers cleared away.

"Another day it is," I said. "And I do mean it. Please have tea with me, when it's convenient."

Owen set his camera bag on the table and stepped toward me, taking my still-gloved hand in his and gravely bowing over it. "I would be honored."

I felt an inclination to giggle, but managed to suppress it. It was a good thing that Owen had a partner.

Of course, I had no idea of the terms of that relationship. It was none of my business. One thing was certain, I would *never* do anything that might hurt Julio.

Not to mention Tony.

"Perhaps Friday?" Owen said, recalling me to the moment.

"Oh—Friday isn't good. We'll be apartment-hunting, and I don't know how long it'll take. How about next week some time?"

"Delightful. We'll compare dates electronically."

"Thanks."

He released my hand, which I'd forgotten he was still holding, and turned to pick up his bag. Julio appeared in the open hall doorway.

"You finished?" he asked.

He'd been waiting for Owen. Normally he would have left by now.

"Yes, just now," Owen said, picking up his folio.

"It took longer than I expected," I said. "I hope you weren't bored, Julio."

"Nah, I did some planning for next week. Not a problem."

Julio smiled to reassure me, then exchanged a look with Owen that had more layers to it than I could interpret. I pulled off my gloves, feeling self-conscious. Then I remembered I still had to put the letters away. I flipped the sides of the napkin over them and picked up the whole thing.

"Thanks again, Owen," I said, moving toward the door. "See you Thursday, Julio."

"Good night," he said.

And night it was, or rather evening, as I stepped into the hall. The daylight was all but gone from the lights around the front door. I looked in on the gift shop and noted that some of the displays needed replenishing, which meant shoppers were buying. Good news for business. I headed upstairs.

Loud yowls greeted me as I stepped into my office. The kitten had her face pressed against the screen wall of the playpen.

"Oh, sweetie, I'm sorry! It took longer than I thought."

I set the letters on my desk and hastened to attend to the kitten. Her litter box needed work, she had stepped in her water dish, and most of all (she informed me), she was hungry. Dealing with these needs took a few minutes. Once she was peacefully gobbling some food, I returned my attention to the letters. I locked them in my desk, napkin and all, and put the gloves in with them for good measure.

Kris stepped in, coat on and bank bag in hand. She deposited a fistful of lavender message slips in my in box. "Don't feel too sorry for her. Dee and Rosa took turns playing with her all afternoon."

"Well, that's good." Kris's expression was unreadable, so I added, "I hope they didn't bother you."

"Not much. I'm off. See you tomorrow."

"Thanks, Kris," I said as she left.

Seated at my desk, I could just see the kitten, still contentedly munching. I looked through the message slips. Three of them were from Tony. Only one had a message, suggesting we have dinner that night.

My cell was in my suite. Hoping I wasn't too late, I picked up the office phone and called him.

"Babe. I was about to give up."

"Sorry—I was away from my desk all afternoon. Have you already eaten?"

"No, and I'm starving."

"Me, too," I said, noticing that the cat's food smelled a little appetizing. "Want to meet at La Choza?"

"Sounds good."

New Mexican food was comfort food, and usually didn't take long to arrive. La Choza was linked to The Shed, its owners descended from the same family, but it was easier to get into. It wasn't too far from the tearoom and closer to Tony's place. I checked on the kitten, then fetched my purse, phone, and coat from my suite.

Downstairs was silent, with the staff gone

and only the lights in the gift shop windows shining faintly out into the hall. I turned on the back porch light and locked up, then drove to the restaurant.

Tony had arrived before me and was waiting in a short queue for a table. He greeted me with a swift hug.

"What were you up to all day? I texted you a bunch."

"Oh, sorry—I haven't looked at my phone. I had Owen come to do some photography, and it took all afternoon."

Tony's eyebrows went up. "Were you modeling?"

"No, no. He was photographing the Captain's letters, and I was handling them."

He nodded. I had told him about the letters, but we hadn't discussed them much. Tony wasn't terribly interested in Captain Dusenberry's murder, which he called the coldest case in New Mexico.

We were now next in line. The host picked up a couple of menus and gave us a "follow me" smile. He led us through the bar to a dining room in the back, where a nice fire was going in a kiva fireplace. The smell of fresh corn tortillas made my mouth water.

A waiter arrived promptly and took our order, and the margaritas showed up with pleasing swiftness. Tony raised his glass, and I picked mine up as well.

"Here's to finding a great apartment."

He nodded and we drank. Salt and lime and tequila lit up my mouth, both delighting and reminding me of my hunger. I took a tortilla chip from the basket, broke it in half, and dipped a piece in the salsa.

"Anything I need to know from your texts?" I asked. I didn't like to take out my phone at the dinner table. Miss Manners had said it was rude, and I agreed.

"Nah," Tony said, and took another swig of his drink. "I got Friday off."

"Good. We can make an early start. Want to spend the night Thursday?"

He gave me a skeptical look.

"We'll leave before the staff gets there."

"Doesn't Julio come in at five or some godawful time?"

"Most of the staff," I amended.

"Hm. Maybe I should just come over early. I can grab a paper and we can look it over before we head out."

"OK."

It made sense to look through the ads and plan which ones to visit. Easier to do that ahead of time than while driving around.

"How's work this week?" I asked.

"Pretty quiet. Waiting on some lab results. Doing some interviews. How about you?"

"The gift shop is doing well. We're getting used to it. Everyone likes it. It's been pretty quiet for us, too, which is good. I've been distracted by the kitten."

"Kitten?"

"Oh, I didn't tell you. I found a kitten by the back door Sunday night, after you'd gone. Poor little thing was freezing, so I brought it in."

"You've got a cat?"

"Just until I can find a home for her."

Tony took a pull on his margarita. "Good, because the Health Department won't approve."

"She's staying upstairs. I got a little playpen for her."

"Careful. You may end up keeping her."

"Well, I can't keep her at the tearoom."

Tony took a chip and scooped it full of salsa, chewed it thoughtfully, and swallowed. "Are we looking for places that allow pets now?"

His tone was neutral, and his face was unreadable. I sipped my drink.

"Do you dislike cats?"

Tony shrugged. "Make it harder to find a place."

"I know. I don't suppose Angela would like a kitten?"

"You'd have to ask her. Between school and

Abuela, she doesn't have a lot of spare time."

Or money, probably. Cat food, litter, vet bills —Angela might not be able to afford it.

Our dinners arrived, and we dropped the subject of the kitten. I was glad, because I didn't want to discuss (or think about) the option of taking her to the shelter. I just didn't want to have to do that. She deserved a forever home.

I had ordered *rellenos,* and dug in. Green chiles stuffed with cheese, battered and deep fried so the cheese melted and ran out into the sauce and made a gooey, fabulous mess. I ate half of one before slowing down. The chile had my whole mouth burning. I sipped some water, then took a hit of my margarita.

"I had lunch with Gina," I said. "She asked me to find out who's your best man and put them in touch."

Tony looked up sharply. "Oh. OK. I'll let you know."

"There was something else she wanted me to ask you. Trying to remember." I frowned, gazing at the fireplace, unwilling to pull out my phone and look at the list Gina had texted me. I thought back over lunch, hoping to jog my memory.

"She wants us to decide where the wedding will be. The sooner we book, the better."

"Not Eldorado, please."

"No. They don't have a garden."

Tony kicked back the last of his margarita. I wondered why he disliked Eldorado. He'd dealt with a messy murder case that had happened at a wedding. Maybe it had been there?

"I'll do some surfing," I said. "It probably doesn't have to be huge. Do you plan to invite a lot of guests?"

He shook his head. "Just the family. A few friends."

I nodded. "Same. We should make a list."

"Yeah. Not tonight."

"Soon, though."

"OK."

The waiter joined us just as I savored my last bite of *relleno.* "Another round?"

Tony shook his head, then looked at me. "You want dessert?"

"Share some flan?"

Tony nodded and glanced at the waiter, who picked up our empty glasses. "I'll have that right out for you."

A busser cleared away our plates. He must have been watching. This place ran efficiently, I thought with approval.

My gaze drifted to the fire, crackling cozily nearby. The chile made a warm glow in my belly, and the margarita had relaxed all my cares away. A few bites of caramelized custard would be the perfect finish.

I could feel Tony watching me. I met his gaze. He looked vaguely concerned, an expression that was not uncommon for him. I reached for his hand and the slight frown melted away.

"I hope we find a place Friday," I said. "That will make everything easier."

"Yeah." His hand tightened on mine.

"Oh, I remember the other question. How formal do you want to be?"

"At the wedding?"

"Yes. Do you want to wear a tux?"

His gaze shifted, getting distant, as if he hadn't considered the question. Then he grinned. "Do you want to wear a Cinderella dress?"

"Um, no. But a *nice* dress. Something elegant." Something I could wear again, to the opera maybe.

"Lace," he said softly, eyelids drooping.

"Lace is nice."

The waiter appeared with our flan, and waited discreetly while we released hands. He set the plate between us, laid two spoons on it, and quietly left.

I took a bite, savoring the silky mouth-feel of the custard, the nip of not-quite-burned caramel. "Silk is nice, too."

"Silk and lace," Tony said, watching me as he ate a bite of flan.

"Mm."

I probably had something in my closet that would do, but I wanted a new dress for the wedding. That, and having the ceremony outdoors, were the two things I'd insist on.

Gina was probably thinking Cinderella. She'd get over her disappointment.

I put Gina out of my thoughts for the moment. Tony had gone quiet and intense. We finished our dessert, paid the bill, and he escorted me to my car.

"Come over for a nightcap?" I asked.

"Yes," he said. His voice had a husky overtone.

He followed me on his bike. All was still, bare branches of the trees reaching toward the sky full of stars. We went in and hurried upstairs, Tony stripping off his gloves and jacket on the way.

"Mew!"

I paused at the top of the stairs. Tony stopped and looked at me.

"Let me check on her. It'll just take a moment."

He followed me to the office doorway and stood watching as I gave the kitten some kibble and a couple of scritches. She settled down to eat and I zipped the playpen closed.

Tony stepped back, letting me lead the way across to my suite. I unlocked it and we went in, tossing aside coats, then clothing. Tony reached for me, hands brushing over my skin, raising goosebumps as he pulled me into his embrace and kissed me. We tumbled into bed.

After a while, lying lazily together, I heard a distant "mew." Ignored it. It came again.

"Mew. Mew."

Tony sighed.

"Want to come meet her?"

He glanced sidelong at me. "Do I have a choice?"

"There's always a choice."

I rose, went to my wardrobe, and selected a satin negligee trimmed with lace. I held it over my head and let it slide down onto my shoulders. A glance at Tony told me I had his attention. I smiled and went to tend to the kitten.

She wanted to play. I dangled the ribbon for her—still her favorite toy—and then dangled it over the ring-ball toy. She made the transition happily, rattling the ball around and around the ring.

I glanced up and saw Tony standing naked in the doorway of my office, a sight I would not soon forget. I went to him.

"Silky," he said, his hands sliding over my back.

"Mm."

He drew me back to bed, and we made love

slowly, thoroughly. At last we lay quietly together, his fingers found my engagement ring, toying with it. I smiled as I drifted toward sleep.

4

I WOKE ALONE. Tony had managed to slip out of bed, dress, and leave without disturbing me. I lay still at first, remembering our evening together. Finally the smell of baking sweets roused me out of bed. I showered and dressed, fed the kitten, and went downstairs to ask Hanh for some extra pastries to take to my appointment with Mr. Hidalgo.

"It's not 'til tomorrow morning," I said. "You could do them at the end of the day."

Han's expression of mild disapproval softened. "OK."

"Do you have everything you need for today? Ramon's coming in, right?"

"Yes. Should be no problem."

"All right. Thanks, Hanh."

She nodded, already focused on the mixer

again. Her long black ponytail reminded me of Owen's. I got out of her way, stopping in at the butler's pantry where Iz was filling the big urn with water to heat for tea. As always, she looked neat as a pin in her lavender dress and white apron.

"Good morning, Iz. How's it going?"

"Fine, thank you." She gave me a fleeting smile.

"Have you seen the gift shop?"

This was the first day she'd come in this week. She shook her head.

"Not yet. I'll go look after this is full."

I left her to it and went to the gift shop myself. The Valentines display looked sparse, and the cupboards underneath it were still empty, so I went upstairs to bring down some merchandise. Nat arrived while I was unpacking more of the black mugs I didn't care for—apparently they were a hit with my customers—and helped me replenish the display.

"Can you come in early on Friday and stand in for me?" I asked her. "I'm taking the day off."

She gave me a look of mock surprise. "Ellen is taking a day off?"

"Tony and I are going house-hunting. We're starting early."

"Ah. Yes, I can come in around nine, if that's early enough."

"That would be great."

She broke down an empty box and folded it for the recycling bin. "What part of town are you looking at?"

"As close to the tearoom as we can afford."

She nodded. "Good luck."

"Thanks. We'll need it."

Iz joined us, and the displays were soon fully stocked. Since there was room to store more merchandise under the new display, I asked her to come upstairs with me and bring down some boxes.

Kris had arrived and was sitting at her desk. She had on a black velour dress and knee-high black boots. Her only ornament, as usual, was the jet beaded necklace she'd worn since Gabriel had died.

"We're going to need some more of those mugs with the big hearts," I said, as Iz came out of the storeroom with the last box of them.

Kris nodded. "Anything else?"

"Valentine cards. And the little heart-shaped china boxes—those are going fast."

"OK."

A loud yowl came from my office. Iz froze in the doorway, eyes wide with alarm.

"It's just the kitten," I said, hurrying past her. "I'll take care of her."

The yowl came again, a piteous sound, a

"something's wrong" sound, not just "pay attention to me." I hurried to the playpen and saw that the kitten had a claw hooked high up on the screen wall. She was tugging at it, which didn't help.

"It's OK," I told her. "Here, let me fix it."

I opened the roof zipper and unhooked her, then cuddled her to calm her down. I stood and turned to speak to Iz, but she was gone. The kitten gave a tiny, mournful mew. I paced the office for a little while, holding her, petting her, talking to her. Finally she began to purr. After another minute I put her back in the playpen and went to look for Iz.

She was in the pantry, setting up china for the day, referring to the reservations list and grouping plates, cups, saucers, and silverware onto trays. I watched, remembering how we had developed this process out of the more haphazard way we had operated when the tearoom first opened.

"I'm sorry the kitten startled you," I said.

"It's OK," she said.

"Do you not like cats?"

She was silent for a moment, then said, "My mom's allergic."

"Ah. Well, I'll let you get on with this."

I waited for a few seconds, then left her alone, heading back to the gift shop. Maybe she had something against cats? I didn't think I'd ever seen a cat at a pueblo, come to think of it. Reservation dogs were the cliché in New Mexico —usually your basic brown mutt. I'd seen plenty of rez dogs, but no rez cats. Was there a tradition I didn't know about?

There were *plenty* of Pueblo traditions I didn't know about. I was born here, but their culture—cultures, the tribes had variations— were different than mine.

Nat was off somewhere. The displays were now full, sparkling with hearts. A lot of pink and red. Not my colors, but that was fine. Seasonal merchandise moved well, and I liked acknowledging the changing times of year. Valentine's Day was going to be big for us.

I stashed the rest of the boxes in the new cabinet space and stood back to look around. The pastry display was empty, having been tidied at the end of the previous day by the servers. It was a little early to fill it yet. I made a couple more trips upstairs to bring down merchandise, until the new cabinets were pretty full. By then it was less than an hour until opening, and I decided to have a break for tea.

Oh, and breakfast. I had forgotten that. I wandered back to the kitchen to see if I could snag a couple of scones. All the stair-stepping had made me hungry. I should get one of those

things that counted how many steps you took—
except I didn't like wearing gadgets on my wrist.
Even watches. I preferred my grandmother's
locket watch.

Nat was not in the kitchen, but Ramon had
joined Hanh there, and stood cutting out scones
at the work table. He glanced up at me with a
smile very like his sister Rosa's.

"Good morning, Ramon. Would you like
some extra hours in February? I was thinking
guitar music would be nice for Valentine's Day,
and maybe the rest of that week."

His eyes widened. Beyond him, Hanh
glanced up at me, disapproving.

"All day?" Ramon asked.

"Just four to six, I think, except for
Valentine's Day. That day you could play as
many hours as you like."

Hanh's frown dissipated. I would not be
cutting into Ramon's kitchen hours.

"Um, sure. Yeah. Let me think about
Valentine's Day."

"Did you have plans?"

"Not really. I'm just not sure about playing
all day."

"Whatever you're comfortable with. We're
already booked solid, so it won't make a
difference to reservations. I just thought it would
be nice to add some live music. Romantic stuff,

you know."

He nodded. "I'll let you know."

I snagged a scrap of scone dough and popped it in my mouth. Ramon grinned.

Music would be a gift to my guests on Valentine's Day, something to make the occasion even more memorable. It would also be a gift to Ramon, who could use the extra pay. I could have omitted the music and made more profit, but by enhancing the quality of the celebration, I knew I'd increase customer loyalty. A worthwhile investment.

A timer went off. Hanh, hands full of pastry, glanced toward the oven.

"I'll get it," I said, grabbing a kitchen towel.

Two large trays of custard tarts gave off a heavenly scent as I set them on the counter to cool. My stomach growled.

"Are there enough for me to have one?" I asked Hanh. "Quality control," I added, grinning.

"You skipped breakfast again," she accused.

I hung my head. "Guilty."

"You can have one." She took an orange from a hanging basket and handed it to me.

"Thank you," I said meekly, then fetched a small plate from the pantry and collected a tart. I took it upstairs to my suite, where I sliced up the orange to go with it. Checking the samovar, I found that Kris had made a pot of Irish Breakfast, for which I was grateful. I poured a cup and sat by the front window in the hall, watching clouds drift by the western horizon, beyond the rooftops of Santa Fe.

This quiet time was the calm before the storm. February was shaping up to be as busy as December had been. I soaked up the peace, knowing I'd have fewer chances in the coming weeks.

The custard tart was still warm. Perfection. I savored it slowly, alternating small bites with slices of orange and sips of tea. The angle of the sun was fairly high; we'd be opening soon.

I saved one bite of tart for the last, letting the custard slide along my tongue, smooth and sweet and delightful. Sighing in contentment, I drank the last sip of tea and sat thinking of how lucky I was, how grateful I was, to be here and to have these wonderful gifts: a beautiful view, delicious food, good tea, and a home of my own.

The home would be changing soon, a mildly uncomfortable thought. I disliked moving, but finding a place that Tony and I could share was essential. Our marriage wouldn't work without it.

Our marriage. Those words were unfamiliar —a little intimidating, if only because the idea was still new.

I stood, collected my dishes, washed them up, and went into my office to check for messages. The kitten peered at me through the screen windows of the playpen.

"Mew."

"Aw, are you lonely? No one to play with?"

She mewed again, and it turned into a yawn, her little pink tongue curling. I crouched and gave the ring toy a tap, as it was against the wall of the pen. The ball rattled, and the kitten attacked it.

"A proper familiar, I see," came a male voice from behind me.

I jumped, turning to see who it was, and fell right on my behind. Owen, in the doorway, struggled not to laugh.

"I caught you off-guard," he said, stepping forward and offering a hand. "My apologies."

I took his hand and he pulled me to my feet, quite easily for someone so slender. He had hidden strength.

"Thank you." I brushed my skirt, slightly embarrassed. I now recalled hearing footsteps on the stairs a moment earlier, but I'd assumed it was someone from my staff.

"I just came to bring you this." He reached into his pocket and held out a thumb drive. "Your photos. There's one folder with everything in it, and another with what I consider the best shots of each letter."

"*Thank* you! That must have taken some time."

He shrugged, sending a shimmer through the sweater he was wearing. It was dark gray, and looked like thick chenille. His hair was caught back in a ponytail again, accentuating the lines of his face.

"I had to check for bad shots anyway – I deleted those. When did you get the kitten?"

"Oh, well...." I told him the story, watching for any sign of personal interest in the cat. I didn't detect anything beyond politeness.

"I don't want to take her to the shelter," I concluded, "but I'm not having any luck finding her a home."

"Maybe you're her new mom."

I sighed, looking down at the playpen, where the kitten was still batting the ball back and forth in the ring. "That would make it even harder to find an apartment."

"But you do like her."

"Oh, she's adorable! But I can't keep her here, in the tearoom."

"Sounds like a quandary."

"It is."

He smiled. "I'll let you get back to work, after I discharge one more errand. Julio and I would like to invite you and Tony to dinner at our place on Saturday."

Astonished, I gaped for a second, then collected myself. "That's very kind of you! I'll have to check with Tony."

"Of course. Just let us know." He gave a formal little nod, added, *"Au revoir,"* and left.

"Au revoir," I answered, slightly late.

I stood gazing at the empty doorway. Owen's presence had begun to unsettle me lately. He seemed not to fit, somehow, in the world that I knew.

Maybe it was just his manners. He was meticulously polite, unusual in this day and age. Some of his turns of phrase were also a bit arcane, almost as if he had come from another time. I happened to like old-fashioned manners and language, so I wasn't quite sure why I found them unnerving in Owen.

Nat stepped into the space I was staring at, coming from Kris's office. "Lucky you," she said, grinning. "I bet Julio is making grand plans to impress you with dinner!"

"Oh, there you are," I said.

"Kris and I just went over the gift shop inventory. She's putting together an order."

"A big order." Kris joined her, teacup in hand, which she filled from the pot atop the samovar. She set the pot on the table. "I've killed the tea."

"I'll make more." I put the thumb drive on my desk and collected the pot.

"I'll go down and watch the gift shop," Nat said.

"Thanks."

I rinsed out the pot and put in more Irish Breakfast, letting it brew while I plugged Owen's thumb drive into my computer and copied over the photos. I brought one up to check it. A perfect image of a letter, legible. I felt relief, knowing they were now documented and would not be lost if something happened to the originals.

Which I needed to take back to the bank. I'd go tomorrow, on my way to meet Mr. Hidalgo. I'd have to print copies of the letters for him today. Maybe in the afternoon.

The tea timer went off, and I poured Kris a cup before setting the pot on the samovar. I made sure the kitten had kibble and water, then went downstairs.

We were open. Most of the alcoves were already occupied by patrons who had come for an early tea, and several shoppers were browsing the gift shop. One of them asked Nat about getting just a cup of tea, and I listened while Nat gently persuaded her to try a cream tea. As Nat led her back to the dining parlor, I took up the "hostess" station at the counter by the register.

The pastry case was now filled with cookies and apple turnovers. The bells on the front door jangled as more customers came in. We were off and running.

It wasn't until early in the afternoon when Dale came in—looking dapper in gray slacks, a subtly brocaded dark green vest over a dove-gray dress shirt, and a gunmetal satin bow tie—that I had time to go up and print out the letters for Mr. Hidalgo. I decided to print them front and back on the same page, which took a bit of time to set up. They were finally all done by four-o'clock. I put all the copies into a large envelope.

Done. That felt good. I looked through my messages. Gina had texted, asking if I'd contacted Angela about shopping for dresses. Wincing, I texted back that this Saturday wouldn't be good. Maybe next week.

Nothing else was crucial. I sent Tony a text about the dinner invitation from Julio and Owen, and went downstairs to collect the pastries for Mr. Hidalgo.

Mick was at the dish-washing station. He gave me a wave and kept on working. Hanh had left, but there was a white square box on the counter with a sticky-note on top, bearing my name in Hanh's brisk handwriting. I peeked inside: two pear galettes and two custard tarts. Perfect.

As I headed back upstairs with the box, I met Nat in the hall, shrugging into her coat. "I'm off," she said. "Dee and Rosa have things under control. See you tomorrow."

"Thanks, Nat."

We exchanged an air smooch, and I went up the stairs and stashed the pastries in my suite. I headed toward my office, but saw that the kitten was sleeping in her playpen, and backed out, going into Kris's office instead.

She held out a lavender message slip as I sat in her guest chair. I took it: a call from Tony. I glanced toward my office, where I'd left my cell phone.

"Let her sleep," Kris said. "You can call back on my line if you want."

"Thanks. Did it sound urgent?"

She shrugged, and stood. "He didn't say it was. I'm going down to get the receipts."

Left alone, I reached for Kris's desk phone and called Tony. Got voicemail.

"Tag, you're it," I said. "I'm free for dinner tonight, if you're asking."

Kris returned with the bank bag, which was bulging pleasantly. She emptied its contents onto her desk and started organizing them for the deposit. A rattle sounded from my office; the ring toy. "I knew it was too good to last," Kris remarked as I stood.

"I'm sorry. Has that been bothering you?"

"Don't worry about it. It's temporary, right?" She gave me a pointed look.

"Yes," I said, and retreated to my office.

The kitten paused and looked up at me. I took her out of the playpen and sat with her on the chaise longue. She settled into my lap and commenced purring loudly. I scritched her ears. I'd better make a vet appointment. She might be chipped! Though I doubted it—if she had a family, they would not have left her outside in a snowstorm. Or if they had, they didn't deserve to get her back.

I was getting attached.

My cell phone rang, on my desk. The kitten startled and tried to leap off my lap. I caught her, and her needle claws sank into my wrist. I gasped, dumped her in the playpen and zipped it shut, and hurried to get to the phone.

It was Tony.

"Hi," I said, a little breathlessly, examining my wrist. A tiny pinprick of blood; I wiped it away.

"I can't do dinner tonight, sorry," Tony said. "A new case came in, and I need to get as much done as possible before Friday."

"It's OK. What about dinner Saturday? Are

you free?"

A pause. "What's it about?"

"About? It's a dinner invitation. Julio and his roommate."

"Yeah, I know. Just wondering why."

"No particular reason. It's just social. Nat thinks Julio wants to impress me with his cooking."

"Not necessary."

"You're right. But it's sweet of him. Do you have a problem with the date? I should let them know..."

"No," Tony said after a second.

"OK. I'll accept, then."

He was silent. I waited a moment, wondering what was bothering him.

"Is the new case making you crazy?" I asked.

"Nothing complicated. Mostly a lot of footwork."

"Well, I hope it goes smoothly. Will I see you tomorrow night?"

"Probably not."

"Friday morning, then."

"Yeah."

"You'll bring the paper."

"Right."

He'd gone monosyllabic. A sign he was done talking.

"OK," I said. "See you then. Love you."

Silence. He'd hung up.

Sighing, I glanced over at the playpen, where the kitten was snoozing again. I got up quietly and went downstairs.

The tearoom's day was ending. Two people chatted softly over cream tea in the dining parlor. A party of four was finishing their afternoon tea in Lily. A few people were browsing in the gift shop. Dale was ringing up a sale of some pastries for one of them. I toyed with the idea of inviting Dale up to meet the kitten, but he didn't seem like the pet-keeping type to me.

I retreated to the hall. Outside, dark was falling. I stepped to the front door to look out of the lights surrounding it. The sky was glowing that particular, magical, twilight blue that I so adored. Such a glorious color, and so fleeting.

So many of life's wonders were fleeting. Would we love them as dearly if they were more permanent? Perhaps we'd take them for granted. I paused a minute longer, taking in that amazing blue, before going back upstairs to the more mundane tasks awaiting me on my desk.

Thursday morning the sun shone brightly as I drove to the bank. The sky was bright blue, the sun had softened all the edges of the snow, and the city was uncrowded but still bustling with energy. Everyone could feel that Spring was approaching.

I returned the letters to the protection of my deposit box, along with the thumb drive with Owen's photos, and drove to the street behind Hidalgo Plaza, where I hoped to find a parking place. Fewer tourists in town; I scored a great space right behind the plaza, and hurried through the sleeping garden with my envelope full of copied letters and my white pastry box.

I passed the stairs to the balcony and knocked at the office, shivering a little while I waited in the shade of the *zaguan*. Through the door's window I saw Mr. Hidalgo emerge from the back office and make his way forward. His gray hair was combed back from his high forehead, and he had on an argyle sweater vest over his white shirt. A thunderbird bolo necktie nestled in the V-neckline of the vest.

"Good morning," he said, smiling as he opened the door wide. I stepped in, returning the smile.

"Good morning. I brought you a little treat." I offered the pastry box. "Thank you for taking time to see me."

"You didn't have to do that!" His eyes lit with pleasure as he opened the box. "Those are too pretty to eat!"

"Oh, but they must be eaten," I countered,

smiling. "That's their whole purpose of existence."

He grinned at me. "I better eat them, then. Come on back."

He led me into his cozily cluttered office and gestured toward a worn leather guest chair. It creaked as I sat in it, but it was quite comfortable.

"You want some coffee?" Mr. Hidalgo asked.

"No, thank you," I said, remembering the tepid coffee in a styrofoam cup that I'd had on a previous visit.

He set the pastries aside on top of a filing cabinet and sat behind the desk. "So you want to talk some more about Tía Maria."

I looked at the photos on the wall behind him, one of which was Maria's. "Yes. You mentioned she turned down a lot of suitors. I wondered if any of them stood out in any way."

He tilted his head, gazing at me. "There is one letter that has raised some questions, but we don't have answers for them. Maria hid it in the back of her diary."

So the family knew about that letter. I felt relieved. Maybe I wouldn't need to confess that I'd sneaked a photo of it with my phone.

"Oh?" I said politely.

"It seems to be from one of her suitors, and it implies that she was interested in him but her father disapproved. There's no indication that she responded."

"Maria didn't keep copies of her own letters?"

He shrugged. "Maybe she did, but she must have destroyed all her correspondence before she died. We never found any of her letters."

A fleeting hope that I might see more of the captain's letters to Maria gently died. It made perfect sense that Maria would have destroyed his letters—all but the one hidden in her diary.

"Can I ask why you're so interested in Maria?" Mr. Hidalgo leaned his elbows on his desk, hands lightly clasped before him as he gazed at me in curiosity.

I took a deep breath. "A little over a year ago, I bought an historic house a couple of blocks to the west of here. It was built as officer's quarters for Fort Marcy Post."

Mr. Hidalgo nodded. "The U.S. Army post."

"Yes. The officer for whom it was built was Captain Samuel Dusenberry."

"Samuel?" Mr. Hidalgo's gaze sharpened.

"Yes," I continued. "Last year I found some letters hidden underneath the floor in my dining room. This week I had them photographed, and I made copies for you."

I handed him the large envelope. His hand reached to open it, then he paused. "Samuel was the name of the suitor who wrote the letter we found."

I nodded, making no comment.

Mr. Hidalgo opened the envelope and pulled out the stack of letters. I had arranged them in chronological order. He looked at the first one, and his eyes went wide.

"This is Maria's handwriting!"

"Yes. These letters were written by Maria to Captain Samuel Dusenberry."

"Oh!" He sifted through the first few pages, as if confirming that they were all Maria's writing, then turned the first page over and peered at the address on the back. "Santa Maria! This is a treasure!"

"Yes, an historic treasure. I plan to donate the letters to the history museum, eventually. I wanted to share them with you first."

"Thank you! Thank you!"

I sat back, watching him pore over the first letter, which was written in Spanish. He devoured it, turned it over and read the back again, then moved on to the next letter. I watched him read the first few pages, happy that he valued the letters as much as I did.

He seemed to realize suddenly that I was still there, and pushed the stack away from him slightly. "There's a lot here."

"Yes. I have not had all the Spanish letters

translated. My Spanish isn't quite good enough to do it. Perhaps you can enlighten me about them, after you've gone through them all."

"This is the Samuel that was Maria's suitor," he said.

"I believe so. It's very clear from this correspondence that they had an affectionate relationship." An understatement, but I was trying to maintain respect for Maria's dignity.

"Do you know what happened?" he asked. "Did she cut it off in obedience to her father?"

"These letters don't indicate that. I've been doing some research and learned that the captain hired a coach for a certain Saturday in April of 1855. I believe he intended that they would elope in it, but he was murdered two days before."

"Murdered? Dios!"

"He was shot in the back. I'm trying to figure out who killed him."

Mr. Hidalgo looked at me, his face showing concern and confusion. I swallowed and cleared my throat.

"Some of the later letters refer to a Reynaldo, who apparently disapproved."

"Maria's brother," he said at once.

"Would you mind my asking if Reynaldo owned a Colt Navy pistol?"

He froze for a second. "Yes," he said. "He did."

"Do you still have it, by any chance?"

He nodded slowly.

Hallelujah! Note to self: get that metal detector and see if there are bullets in the wall of the dining parlor.

"There's no way to prove it was the gun that killed your Samuel," he added.

"There might be," I said. "You see, he was shot in the house. My house. In the room where I found these letters, in fact."

Frowning now, Mr. Hidalgo acknowledged this with a nod.

"And I think one or both of the bullets may have lodged in the walls. They're adobe," I added. "There was an investigation, but the bullets were never found."

"They would not have proved anything," Mr. Hidalgo said.

"Back then, no. But modern ballistics could now identify whether they came from a certain gun."

"You want to examine Reynaldo's gun."

I held up a hand. "I haven't found the bullets. Until I do, there's no point, although I'd love to just see the gun."

"It's in storage. I can get it out and show it to you another day."

I nodded, relieved that he was willing to do that. "Thank you. I'd like that very much."

"Reynaldo would not have killed him," Mr. Hidalgo added.

"How do you know?" I asked gently.

His hands lay atop the letters. For a moment one of them tightened, as if to make a fist, then he deliberately relaxed the fingers and laid them flat. "Reynaldo was a good man. An honorable man."

I nodded. The Hidalgos might be biased on that subject, but I let it pass.

"He would never have shot a man in the back."

Oh. That was a valid point.

"I see," I said. "Then, if I do find the bullets, a ballistics test would prove that Reynaldo didn't kill the captain."

"You don't have to do a test to prove that."

"I'm curious, though. Would you be willing, if I find the bullets?"

He hesitated briefly. "Yes, if it would ease your mind." He glanced down at the letters. "You have given us a tremendous gift."

I smiled. "I'll leave you to enjoy them, but I'd like to ask one more question today."

"Anything," he said, gazing in amazement at the stack of letters.

"Maria owned a gold locket. She's wearing it in that photo." I nodded toward the picture of Maria on the wall. "Do you still have it?"

"Yes," said Mr. Hidalgo.

Abruptly he stood and went to one of the two filing cabinets. He took a ring of keys from his pocket, unlocked the cabinet, and took out a steel box which he set on the desk. This he unlocked with another key. He pulled out a small piece of black velvet, which he laid between us on the desk. Then he took a coin envelope from the box and removed a gold locket, hanging from a pin. With careful reverence, he laid it on the velvet.

I leaned forward to look at it. The pin was a straight bar, but I now saw that it was decorated with filigree, a detail that had not come through in the photograph.

"It's beautiful," I said. "Have you opened it?"

Mr. Hidalgo nodded. He picked up the locket and gently popped it open. Inside was an image of the Virgin of Guadalupe, along with a small, brown ring. It was too thin to be leather. I looked up at Mr. Hidalgo.

"It's a hair ring," he said. "Those Victorians, they liked to make jewelry out of hair."

"Yes," I said looking closely at it. "Often as a remembrance of a loved one. Was Maria's hair brown?"

"It was black."

The ring was a very fine braid, maybe two millimeters thick. I looked up at him. He met my gaze.

"This could be Captain Dusenberry's hair," I said.

"Maybe."

"I believe he gave Maria this locket," I said. "I found a record of him purchasing a gold locket from Seligman's, about a week before he was killed."

Mr. Hidalgo's eyes widened. "Ai," he breathed, looking down at the locket.

"Yes."

"Do you have anything that would give a sample of Samuel's DNA?" he asked.

"I'll look. I have a few of his things."

And there was always the cemetery. Though I rather doubted the caretakers would be willing to exhume a grave to confirm a romance that was a century and a half old. It wouldn't even solve the captain's murder.

"It would be wonderful to know for certain that this was his hair." He carefully put the ring back in the locket and closed it.

"It doesn't bother you that he was an Anglo and wanted to marry Maria?" I asked.

Mr. Hidalgo made a derisive sound. "This is the 21st century. We're past that by now, don't you think?"

I smiled. "Yes. And I confess, I'm quite caught up in this romantic story, though it has a tragic ending."

Mr. Hidalgo smiled back. "We'll have to get to the bottom of it."

"Indeed."

I stood and slung my purse over my shoulder. "Thank you for showing me the locket."

"Thank you for giving me these letters. Such a treasure," he said again, shaking his head as he stood. "Do you think—would you be willing to show me the originals, before you donate them?"

"Yes. They're in my safe deposit box. I can bring them when you have the pistol, and we'll do a show and tell."

And I might even bring more to show, though I hadn't yet mentioned the elopement kit. It was still too new a discovery; I felt possessive.

Mr. Hidalgo accompanied me to the door, where I paused and offered a hand. "I'll search for those bullets and for a DNA sample from the captain. I'll let you know what I find."

He shook my hand, then pulled me close and put his arm around my shoulders. Surprised, I returned the hug gently, feeling the frailty of his frame. He released me and stepped back.

"Thank you, Miss Rosings."

"Ellen," I said.

"Ellen. Then you must call me Eduardo."

"Thank you, Eduardo. I'll talk to you soon."

Outside, I moved into the garden and found a splash of sunlight to stand in. A light breeze stirred bare honeysuckle vines. I gazed toward the center of the *plazuela,* wondering if there had been a garden here in Maria's day or if it was only used to store wagons and stable horses. I preferred to envision a garden—at least a little kitchen garden in one corner, with chickens running about, eating the bugs. As I stood musing, a flash of light caught my eye.

Startled, I looked for the source, but saw nothing obvious. No bright metal objects, no wind chimes or pinwheels.

"Captain?" I whispered. "Samuel?"

Only the breeze sighed in answer. A shiver went through me that had nothing to do with the temperature. I realized I was standing only a short distance from where I had identified Gabriel's body on Halloween night. A few days before then, I'd seen a flash of light here in the *plazuela,* very like the one that had just occurred. Like the gleam from the edge of a moving chandelier drop.

Could the captain have tagged along with me today? If so, had he been pleased to see Maria's locket again?

I hurried through the garden and out the north *zaguan* to where I'd parked my car. I had no answers to those questions.

5

MY CELL PHONE STARTLED ME OUT OF A DREAM the next morning. I caught at the wisps of it... something to do with chickens and stars...as I fumbled for the phone. 6:35. It was Tony.

"I'm on my way over. Just picked up the paper."

"OK," I said, sitting up in bed.

It was still dark outside. No one was going to show us apartments this early.

"Do you have a thermos?"

"Yes."

"You might want to fill it with coffee. I'm bringing mine."

"I'll probably do tea."

"OK. See you in a few."

"Bye."

He was gone. He'd called to wake me. I'd

planned to be awake and ready by the time he arrived, but he'd caught me sleeping in. Drat.

I hurried into some clothes and dealt with the kitten, giving her access to the litter box, then feeding her. I hastily made tea and baked some scones in my toaster oven, since sweet smells from downstairs were driving me crazy. I had just filled my thermos and scarfed the last of the scones when my phone rang again.

"I'm here," Tony said.

"Be right down."

I carried the kitten across the hall and put her in the playpen. "Be good, honey," I said. She mewed softly, as if she understood and was resigned to my leaving. For some reason that tugged at my heart.

I went back for my coat and purse, locked my suite, and hurried downstairs. Julio's salsa music wafted out from the kitchen along with the yummy aromas. I didn't stop to say goodbye; we'd talked on Thursday, and he knew my plans for the day. He and Hanh were the only ones here, so far.

Tony had parked his bike behind the kitchen, leaving the closer spaces for my staff (and perhaps hoping they might not notice the bike). He stood on the portal, breath fogging in the morning cold, hands stuffed in the pockets of his leather jacket and a thermos tucked under one arm.

"Hi," I said, wishing I'd put on a hat and scarf. The day was clear, though, and would warm up quickly now that the sun was rising. I continued to my car, Tony following. We got in and I started the engine, turned the heater to high, and put my thermos in the cup holder by my elbow.

Tony produced a folded page of want ads and opened it. "Got a pen?"

I fished one out of the center console and handed it to him, then put on my gloves.

Our breath was still fogging. I moved the heat to the windshield.

Tony scanned the ads, circled several, then handed the page to me and took out his phone. "I need to look up one address. Not sure where it is."

I glanced through the ads he had marked, impressed that he knew all but one of the street names. Looking through the page, I marked a couple more ads. We could have done this in the dining parlor and stayed warmer, but Tony wanted to get going, apparently.

"OK, let's head for this one," he said. "Take Paseo to St. Francis."

I backed out of my space, turned the car, and drove out into town, following Tony's directions. We crossed St. Francis Drive, one of the main boulevards through town, and headed into a neighborhood that dated back to the 1940s and 50s. Cinder-block houses with stucco, mostly. Fairly well kept. A house would be nicer than an apartment, but I feared the rent would be too expensive.

"That one," Tony said, pointing to a pinkish-brown house with a dirt front yard and a single-car garage. I pulled over to the curb and left the engine running.

It looked a little run down compared to the neighboring houses. Not as bad as the junkyard house we'd looked at last weekend, but it didn't fill me with confidence.

"You could put a garden in the yard," Tony said.

It would take a lot of work, but yes. I could. I eased the car backward a few feet, trying to get a view into the back yard. A big shed behind the garage was all I could see.

"How much?"

Tony read the rent from the ad. I winced.

"Hey, we're probably not going to do better."

"Let's call this a maybe. Can we look at some others?"

"Sure."

He checked the paper and directed me to the next place. It was a duplex, and looked pretty small. The other half had three large dogs in the tiny back yard, which shared a chain-link fence with the vacant side.

We kept looking, until we'd seen all the places we'd marked. None of them was stellar, but a couple had potential.

It was now past 8:00, no longer too early to call on a business day. I parked the car and drank some tea while Tony made a couple of calls. No answer on the first one; the second one agreed to show us their rental in half an hour. Tony made more calls.

We spent the morning revisiting three of the best bets—two apartments and the pink house—meeting the owners and touring the properties. Each had issues.

The first apartment was in a concrete block of a building, gray and uninviting, and had the disadvantage of being surrounded by commercial properties. The manager, a lackluster man in a padded plaid coat, showed us the apartment. We followed him through the rather depressing rooms, but I had already crossed it off my list, and I was relieved when Tony caught my eye and shook his head. The manager seemed unsurprised when we left without asking any questions.

Next up was the pink house. The back yard turned out to be as barren as the front. It looked as if it had been over-grazed by a herd of cattle (probably just worn down by big dogs), and the cinder block wall was crumbling in two places. Inside the house, there were musty smells and I noticed water damage on the ceilings in two rooms. That meant the roof was bad, which meant the owner wasn't taking good care of the place. Also: brown and orange shag carpet.

I caught Tony's eye and glanced up at the water-stained ceiling in the dining room. He followed my gaze and gave a resigned nod. We thanked the owner and left.

The next-best bet was an apartment building about half a mile to the south of the pink house. The manager led us up two flights of steep stairs —outdoors, but semi-sheltered by the building itself—to a tiny, character-free apartment that faced west. No view of the mountains. There would be nice sunsets, maybe, but no good way to see them. If there had been a balcony, that might have increased the appeal, but there was none, not even a window of significant size. The kitchen was tiny, with an elderly electric stove top and skimpy oven. No washer/dryer, and no on-site laundromat. That was a deal-breaker right there, for me. I could take laundry to the tearoom and use the washer/dryer there, but ugh. Two flights of stairs with a laundry basket.

We looked through the ads again and decided to take a look at the duplex. The owner arrived ten minutes after the time she had promised to meet us. Meanwhile I finished the last of my tea and developed an increasing wish that we had stopped for coffee before calling.

The dogs in the back yard of the occupied half of the duplex had barked constantly from the time of our arrival. The owner, a middle-aged woman wearing a down parka that made her look like a pale blue marshmallow, seemed oblivious to them.

She let us into the vacant side of the duplex and showed us around. It was old, of course, with an in-floor heater of which I was dubious. The floors were wood, which was nice, but they badly needed refinishing. The walls were dingy, needing paint. The windows were single-pane, probably original to the house. Small panes, and I could feel the cold pouring off them. This place would be expensive to heat.

The shotgun kitchen was narrow and felt cramped, though it did have a gas range and oven. No dishwasher, though.

"Wanna see the back yard?" The marshmallow lady asked.

"Yeah," Tony said.

"It's right through the mud room."

She led the way through a small room that I thought was probably actually a laundry room, though there was no washer or dryer, and any hookups for such were hidden by a large, empty storage shelf against the interior wall beneath a set of cupboards. Like those in the kitchen, they had been painted so many times all their edges were soft.

As we stepped outside, the dogs threw themselves against the chain link fence separating the two tiny yards, snarling and barking. I backed away; Tony frowned. The yard was a bare rectangle that made the pink house's yard look luxurious, with a disconcerting view of the back porch of someone else's house on the next street over. No refuge here; I couldn't picture myself relaxing in this yard, much less trying to garden.

"OK, thanks," Tony said, and headed inside.

I followed, with the owner bringing up the rear.

"So, you interested?" she said.

"We need to think about it," Tony said.

"You look like nice folks. I'll give you twenty-five off the rent if you take it today."

Tony and I exchanged a glance. I knew by his set jawline that his answer to that would be no.

"We'll talk, and let you know," I told the owner.

"Well, OK, but you better hurry. I got two more calls."

Tony was at the front door. I turned to the owner. "Thanks for your time."

She gave me a disappointed stare as I followed Tony out.

"No way," he said when we were back in the car. "Those dogs are a menace.

"They're rather loud, yes."

"I know a judge who says the worst cases he gets are all barking dog cases."

"Oh. Well, I'm glad, because the utilities would be expensive, I think. Are you hungry?"

"Starving."

"Let's get lunch. Want to try that little Indian place down the street?"

"Anything."

I drove to the restaurant I'd spotted on the way in, a mere two blocks from the duplex. It was in an old house that had been updated with double-pane windows and baseboard heating, and the oak floor had been gorgeously finished. If only the duplex had been given such a treatment! Fabulous aromas surrounded us as we followed a pleasant woman in a canary yellow sari, long black braid falling to her hip, to a tiny table overlooking the winter-sleeping garden.

"Something to drink?" she asked as she settled us with menus.

"Water and some chai for me," I said.

"Same," Tony added.

The chai arrived within two minutes, and I wrapped my hands around the cup to warm them, inhaling the bracing scents of cardamom, ginger, and clove.

Tony pulled out the ads and looked over the rather battered page. He shook his head.

"Today's a bust."

"I agree."

He sipped his chai, appeared to notice it wasn't coffee, and took a larger swallow, nodding approval. "We can try again next week."

I sighed. Doing this every week would quickly become a drain. "You can get off work again?"

He grimaced. "I'll take a half-day."

I nodded, hoping we'd have better luck the next time. I would not be able to keep taking Fridays off. February was going to be busy.

I took a swallow of chai, put down my cup, and picked up the menu, feeling discouraged. Tony's hand found mine.

"Don't worry. We'll find a place."

"I hope so."

"We've got time."

I met his gaze and summoned a smile. He seemed to have more faith than I did, at the moment.

6

IT WAS AFTER DARK. I wept as I searched the empty tearoom frantically, looking under every piece of furniture, in every corner and cupboard, for the kitten.

"Minuit! Minuit!"

I had searched the entire upstairs—even the storage room behind Kris's desk—after finding her playpen empty and open. Now I was making a second circuit of the downstairs. In the dining parlor, I looked under the table, under the sideboard, under the table again, and in the corner where the captain's desk had stood. I wished I had borrowed a cat detector, but there hadn't been time.

Cat detector?

With a gasp of frustration I came awake. Cold light seeped around the edges of the window curtains in my bedroom. It was early, but I knew I wouldn't get back to sleep. I tumbled out of bed and hurried over to the kitty's box.

She was sleeping. Safe and secure.

I sighed with relief, pulled on my robe, and trudged to the kitchenette to make tea. No point in going back to bed. I curled up in my chair with the first cup of Assam, nursing it as I watched the day brighten outside the window.

Not a great start to the weekend.

I drank a second cup, then took a shower and dressed. Scones were baking downstairs; the smell rose up the stairwell and invaded my suite. Determined not to beg breakfast again, I made toast with raspberry jam and devoured it, with more tea, before showing my face downstairs.

"Morning," I said, smiling at Julio and Ramon as I looked in on the kitchen. Hanh had the day off.

"Hi, Ellen," Ramon said. "Can we talk about Valentine's?"

"Sure."

"I know I said I'd play, but..."

I grinned. "You've got a date."

He looked sheepish, and also pleased with himself. "Is it OK if I just play from noon to three?"

"Sure," I said, with only a tiny pang of regret that there wouldn't be music into the evening.

"Thanks."

"I'll play the rest of the week, four to six, like you asked."

"That'll be fine."

"Thanks." He smiled again, then went back to loading a parchment-covered baking sheet with frozen scones.

I stepped over to where Julio was cutting precise triangles out of frozen bread to make the elegant, three-tiered tea sandwiches featured in the January menu. "What time did you want us tonight?"

"Between six-thirty and seven," Julio said. "You don't have to rush."

"Um, I'll need your address."

"Oh, yeah. I'll text it to you."

"Thanks. I'm looking forward to it."

He looked up at me with an enigmatic smile. "Me, too."

Chefs like their surprises. I left him to his work. He'd warned me he'd be taking off a little early that day—and how could I object? It looked like everything was in hand.

I went back upstairs to tie a ribbon around the tiny jar of saffron I'd picked up the previous afternoon to bring as a gift for our hosts. I'd debated the wisdom of buying spice for a chef, but it was high quality saffron and that stuff wasn't cheap. The sort of thing Julio would enjoy, but might not indulge in for himself. I had bought a bottle of lemon-infused olive oil for Nat at the same time, as a thank-you for standing in for me.

Tony had gone back to work after our lunch at the Indian place, which had turned out to be truly excellent. I'd be dining there again—I knew Gina would love it and hoped she hadn't already discovered it.

Yesterday I had deliberately avoided the pile of message slips in my office, deciding that a day off should truly be a day off. Now I went to face them. Stopping in my suite, I found the kitten awake and hungry. I set her up in the playpen for the day, making extra certain that it was closed tightly, then reported to my desk.

Julio's text had arrived on my cell. I looked up the address on a map, and saw that it was on Artist Road, less than ten minutes away. I texted Tony suggesting he arrive at the tearoom by 6:15.

Working my way through returning calls and emails took most of the morning. The most disappointing message was from Mr. Quentin, who very much regretted that he did not have a metal detector to lend me.

Cat detector.

I looked over at Minuit, who was idly batting at a sparkly pom-pom that dangled from the ceiling of the playpen. Pulling my current to-do list toward me, crossed off a couple of things I'd completed, and added "metal detector" and "cat vet date" to the bottom of the list.

Nat was not coming in, so I went back downstairs after finishing the messages, and played hostess until the four-o'clock customers had all been seated. Dee was there by then, and I entrusted her with keeping an eye on the gift shop while I went upstairs to shower and change for the evening.

I chose a long-sleeved knit dress of dark blue and a lovely hand-woven shawl with broad stripes of turquoise, purple, and blue. My mother's silver heishi necklace completed the ensemble. Hair piled loosely atop my head. Knee-high boots because of the cold. I fed the kitten, collected coat, purse, keys, phone and the saffron gift, and locked my suite before going downstairs.

We were closed, but I could hear Dee talking with a couple of lingering customers in the gift shop. Evening was deepening outside the windows. A hint of piñon aroma from the fireplaces gave the house a cozy feeling. I loved this time of day.

I stepped into the unoccupied dining parlor and stood watching out the French doors for Tony's headlight. Snow lingered beneath the

bushes and trees, and along the north side of the
shed and the kitchen. Through the bare branches
of the cottonwoods, above the two-story building
across the next street, I could just see the
mountains, snow-frosted, reaching up to the dar-
kening sky.

What had this view been like in Captain
Dusenberry's day?

There had been another officer's house immediately behind this one, I knew from images
of old maps I had obtained from the archives.
This had been "Officers' Row." My house was
the only one left. Beyond the officers' houses,
the military park had spread toward the east,
with the quartermaster's warehouse over which
Captain Dusenberry had presided, and barracks,
and a parade ground. All wooden, probably. All
gone now. Only the Palace of the Governors—
which had been the military headquarters then,
and was a much older, adobe building—
remained.

So very different. A bit disconcerting that
such a large military institution was now gone,
almost without a trace.

Tony's bike turned up the driveway, its
headlight flashing across the window. I picked
up my coat from the chair over which I had
draped it, and put it on. Going out the back door,
I glimpsed Mick through the kitchen windows,

silently bopping as he dealt with the last of the dishes. I locked the back door behind me and headed for my car.

Tony joined me at the driver's side. "You look great," he said, kissing my cheek. "Smell great, too. Mmm."

I let out an involuntary giggle as he nuzzled my neck. His nose was cold, though his breath was hot.

"We'll be late," I protested.

He stepped back, grinned impishly, and went around to the passenger door. Inside I cranked up the heater and headed for Artist Road, after giving Tony the address. I could find it, but from our house-hunting excursions I knew he enjoyed giving me directions.

"Fancy," he commented, taking out his phone.

That thought had also crossed my mind. I paid Julio well, but not well enough for that neighborhood. Probably not even well enough for half the rent up there. And though Owen was a gifted photographer, I doubted his vocation brought him enough income for such an expensive part of town.

Unless he had his stuff showing in the galleries. That was a possibility, given his circle of friends. I hadn't been to many galleries over the past year.

Cresting the steep rise at the bottom of Artist Road, I saw Santa Fe spread out to the south, glittering in the evening. How lucky Julio was to have such a view!

"Take the next right," Tony said, and I turned onto a small street lined with one-story, Pueblo-style townhouses. Pottery porch lights featured cutouts of zias, thunderbirds, and other Southwestern motifs. I noted license plates from California, Texas, New York and other states in the driveways as I peered at the house numbers, looking for Julio's.

"That one." Tony pointed to a home on the south side of the street. I recognized the black Mercedes in the driveway as Owen's. There wasn't room behind it, so I parked at the curb.

The porch light here was a setting sun with wavy rays. Scraps of snow remained beneath shrubs in the garden, one of which was some kind of weeping evergreen. We stepped onto the porch and Tony pressed the doorbell. The door opened almost instantly.

"Welcome," Owen said, smiling and beckoning us into an entryway from which a hall ran forward into the house. White walls, a domed ceiling, and tile accents around the arched doorways evoked a Spanish feeling. The floor was Saltillo tile.

Owen had on a sleek, dark shirt and a sand-cast concho belt threaded through the loops of black jeans. His long hair was loose over his shoulders.

"Julio's in the kitchen," he added as he closed the door behind us. I had already gleaned this information from the mouth-watering aromas filling the hall. "May I take your coats?"

I offered the saffron jar to free my hands. "This is a little thank-you for the invitation."

Owen smiled, admiring the jar. "The golden spice. A beautiful gift."

Tony stuffed his gloves into a pocket and handed his coat to Owen. Their gazes met and held—for an instant neither moved—and I sensed some masculine non-verbal communication occurring. Owen smiled again, accepted my coat, and nodded toward an archway through which I could see a fire gently flickering in a kiva fireplace.

"Make yourselves comfortable. I'll be right back."

The smell of piñon blended with the fabulous aromas of Julio's handiwork to create an atmosphere of comfort and promised luxury. I stepped into the living room and beheld a picture window overlooking that southward city view, much more impressive here than from the street, as it was unobstructed by any buildings on the hill. I could see the bell towers of the cathedral, and the massive pile of La Fonda. Strings of lights still adorned the trees in the Plaza. I tried to spot the tearoom, but big buildings obscured it.

"Nice view," Tony said beside me.

I tore my gaze away from it and looked at him. He was wearing the sweater that Nat and Manny had given him for Christmas, over a pair of black dress pants. I gave him a smile, then looked around the room.

I had half-expected a Goth motif, but though the light was low and the furniture was black leather, the room was more a blend of classic Santa Fe and Arts and Crafts. A low, *vigas*-and-*latillas* ceiling created the feeling of a cozy cave. Restrained lighting, consisting of multiple candles, the fireplace, and a couple of low table lamps with warmly glowing mica shades, allowed the lights of Santa Fe to dominate the room. A large oriental rug covered most of the tile floor. The result was rich and warm, with mystery in the corners.

One such mystery drew my notice; I had to step closer to confirm that it was indeed a small harp, resting in the arms of an antique chair in the corner near the fireplace. A brass plaque was fixed to the upper end of the curved top part, whatever that was called; I wasn't an expert in harps. I moved closer, trying to read the plaque in the low light.

"It was made in Ireland," Owen's voice said from the far end of the room. "That's what the plate says."

I turned and saw him standing just inside the archway. Tony, between us, stood in the exact center of the rug.

"It's yours?" I asked Owen. "Do you play?"

He gave his slight bow. "I do."

"Will you play something for us?"

"Ah—certainly. Let me just check on Julio."

He went out again. Tony remained in the center of the room, watching me. Yes, a bit of the old dog-guarding-a-bone energy. I decided to ignore it. There were two sofas—one facing the fireplace, the other facing the window—and a Stickley-style armchair, all sharing a gorgeous coffee table made from a slab of what looked like mesquite, its edges twining organically. I chose the window-facing sofa. Tony sat beside me and put an arm around me. Only *slightly* possessive. I relaxed against him, grateful to be at the start of a weekend.

"Can metal detectors be rented?" I asked.

"Probably. Why?"

"I was hoping to borrow one from Mr. Quentin, but he doesn't have one. Do you know anyone who might?"

"Yeah, the crime scene techs."

"I don't suppose...?"

He gave me a skeptical look. "What's it for?"

"I want to find the bullets that killed Captain Dusenberry. I think they may be in the wall of my house."

Tony stifled a sigh. "I can ask."

"It was a murder. So they'd be investigating a crime."

Tony looked at me sidelong. Good—I'd succeeded in distracting him.

Owen returned carrying a small silver tray bearing a slender pottery pitcher and three matching cups with no handles. He set it on the coffee table and picked up the pitcher. "Would you like some mulled wine?"

"Sure," I said, sitting up.

Fragrant steam rose from the pitcher as Owen poured. He handed me a cup and I wrapped my fingers around its warmth, inhaling the aroma of wine, honey, and spices before taking a cautious sip. It was just the right temperature.

"Dinner will be about fifteen minutes," Owen said, offering Tony a cup of wine. Tony accepted and smelled it, looking dubious.

Owen poured for himself, sipped, and smiled, then set the cup on the banco by the fireplace and picked up the harp. Settling into the chair where it had rested, he leaned the instrument against his shoulder and strummed the strings lightly, then launched into an intricate piece that sounded Celtic. With the firelight illuminating the translucent strings, gleaming on the honey-colored soundboard of the harp and lighting subtle glints in Owen's hair, he looked like a medieval bard. Out of place in time, yet again.

He played exquisitely. As a flourishing arpeggio concluded the song, I realized I was holding my breath. I let it go and applauded. After a moment, Tony joined in.

"What other hidden talents do you have?" I asked.

Owen shrugged, smiling. "I'm a dabbler. I do a little bit of a lot of different things."

"Well, you're more than a dabbler on that. You could play professionally."

He shrugged again and picked up his wine. I sipped my own, watching him. Dared I ask if he would play at the tearoom? Just for Valentine's evening?

I was already beholden to him, though, for the photos of the letters. I would pay him, even if I had to nag him for a bill, but I was coming to realize that he probably didn't have to work at all. Which meant that he had taken those photos, and spent hours processing them, as a favor to me.

And he had sort-of agreed to photograph the wedding. Ai.

It had to be Owen who could afford this splendid house. Which implied that he had independent means. If he dabbled in other expensive hobbies—harps, even smaller ones, were not cheap—then he was probably quite comfortable indeed.

Music distracted me; Owen's fingers stroked the harp strings, a whispering glissando, as he gazed distantly at the fire. I suspected he wasn't really seeing the flames. He had gone somewhere, into the place where his music arose. I watched as he began to play, this time a quiet, rainfall sound of softly-plucked strings, long fingers dancing in the firelight.

He was improvising, I realized. Playing from the heart.

I knew just how much skill, and how much courage, it took to play competently that way. Yes, he was a master at this art as well.

Tony moved beside me, distracting me as he leaned forward to set his cup on the coffee table. Reminded of my own, I sipped, then took a larger swallow of the wine, which was cooling. Owen remained oblivious, lost in the music. I turned my head to smile at Tony.

For just a second, I saw dismay in his eyes. I leaned closer to whisper to him. "Maybe he's a changeling."

Tony pulled back, a slight frown of confusion

on his face.

"I mean, how many humans can play like that and also take great photos?"

I admire him, but I'm not hot for him, was what I was trying to say. I hoped Tony understood.

Well, maybe a *little* hot for him, but I would never act on that impulse.

Tony looked back at Owen. I slid my hand into his and felt him relax.

The music gently swelled into a rippling stream. I felt the tensions of the week falling away, assisted by a slight drowsiness from the wine and the warmth of the fire. I leaned my head on Tony's shoulder, watching Owen's hands dance over the strings.

Owen glanced up, and the cascading music drifted to a stop. Lifting my head, I saw Julio standing in the archway.

"Sorry to interrupt," he said, "but dinner's ready."

7

OWEN STOOD AND PUT THE HARP BACK on the chair. Tony and I followed him and Julio across the entryway and through another arch into the dining room. Julio was wearing a long-sleeved burgundy shirt that looked like linen or muslin, over dark slacks. It made him look a bit older than he did in his chef's working togs.

Two candelabra filled the room with gentle light, supplemented by a dome ceiling light—obviously on a dimmer—centered over a long dining table set for four. I recognized a painting on the wall above the chair at the far end of the table, where Owen seated himself. It was a landscape, and it took me a minute to remember where I had seen it—at the autumn art show at the convention center (formerly Sweeney Center). It was one of Gabriel's.

The table could have seated eight, but was set for four. Ample elbow room, which was a good thing as there were three wine glasses— champagne, red, and digestif—at each place, along with a water goblet. Place cards with our names in sweeping calligraphy directed me and Tony to take the middle seats, I with my back to the window, which was curtained. Julio's place was near the door, for easy access to the kitchen.

The centerpiece was a long, low, dark-green ceramic bowl between the candelabra, with white alstroemeria and stargazer lilies tumbling out of it. Tendrils of the weeping evergreen from the front yard accented the flowers and spilled from the bowl to wind around piñon cones resting on the sage-colored tablecloth. The evergreen had small clusters of short needles, a little like rosemary, except that it was more blue. Spruce, perhaps?

White porcelain oriental teacups, each holding a different treat (salted almonds, figs, cherries, kumquats), nestled among the greens. Unusual and colorful, lovely for a winter meal. I nabbed an almond and popped it into my mouth.

The place settings were more formal than I'd expected, with a gold-colored metal charger beneath the gold-rimmed dinner plate (*very* elegant china, and it looked old, perhaps an heir- loom). The silverware implied both a soup

course and a salad course, as well as dessert.
Julio was indeed showing off his skills.

An *amuse-bouche* sat on a tiny black plate in
the precise center of the dinner plate: a single,
small grilled scallop, scarcely bigger than a
sugar cube, adorned with a sliver of chive and
resting on a swirl of pale golden aioli. I admired
the artistic treat as I laid my napkin in my lap.

Julio took a bottle of champagne from a
cooler on a massive Spanish-style sideboard
against the wall behind Tony. An array of other
bottles adorned the sideboard, almost dismaying,
until I realized several of them would be options
for the digestif. Julio filled our flutes, then took
his seat.

Owen picked up his glass. "Health and happiness."

We joined the toast. The champagne was
divine. I let the tingle of the bubbles fade on my
palate before addressing the *amuse-bouche*.
Across the table, Tony was watching me. I
smiled and picked up the tiny seafood fork from
its resting place in the soup spoon. No oyster
here, but the scallop looked even better.

And it was. I speared it with the fork, swept it
through the aioli, and popped it into my mouth.
Warm, with a slight crunch from the grilling, and
the sweet taste of a perfect scallop, followed a
moment later by a bloom of flavor from the aioli:

touch of garlic, hint of lemon, and...

Saffron. I smiled, savoring the blend of flavors and textures, taking my time enjoying the morsel. At last I swallowed and smiled.

"Oh, Julio. That was divine."

He nodded, almost a little bow like Owen's. "Thank you. And thank you for the gift. As you see, it was the perfect choice."

"I'm happy to replenish your stores."

I saw Tony take a scrape of aioli with his tiny fork and eat it. The sauce was worth the effort, but I left my fork where it was, knowing there were many more delights to come.

Julio stood and retrieved a tray from the sideboard, onto which he collected the little black plates and the seafood forks. Moving swiftly and efficiently, he left for the kitchen and returned immediately with a tray of small soup bowls. I sipped my champagne as he served these, beginning with mine. Glancing at it, I saw that it was a cream soup, adorned with shreds of crab.

"So, Tony," said Owen, "are you working on any interesting cases at the moment?"

Tony hesitated. "Yes, but they're not really good for dinner conversation."

"Do you have subordinates to assist you?"

Tony hunched a shoulder, shaking his head. "I have colleagues—mostly with their own specialties. We rely on the uniforms to get things going."

Owen nodded. "First responders."

"Yeah, and regular beat cops. Those guys are the front line."

Julio had resumed his seat, leaving the tray on the sideboard. He and Owen simultaneously picked up their soup spoons, traditionally the signal that permitted guests to do likewise. I took a spoonful. Potato-leek, with more of the crab shreds stirred through. It was rich, and I was glad the portion was small.

Owen continued to ask Tony about his work, which was kind of him. Tony gave brief answers between mouthfuls of soup, which he appeared to be enjoying very much. He finished before anyone else and glanced at my place setting, then followed my lead in where to leave the spoon.

I took my time, savoring the interaction of the flavors with the wine, and enjoying the conversation. Owen was drawing information out of Tony that I hadn't heard before.

"So, as in many businesses, paperwork is the bane of efficiency," Owen remarked. Tony nodded. "Can't tell you how many cases go stale while you're waiting on a warrant or a court date. It's not as bad in my line, for example, but half the traffic cases, for example, expire before they're finished."

"The cost of bureaucracy."

"Yeah."

The conversation continued while Julio silently cleared the soup plates. He was gone for a couple of minutes, then returned with a platter of ribeye steaks, still softly sizzling, from which he invited me to choose.

"That small one, please. Oh, they smell heavenly!"

"It's wagyu," Owen said as Julio laid the steak on my plate. "He won't tell you, but I can say that he spent hours finding the best in the state for you."

Julio grinned. "I owe the head chef at Izanami a bottle of single-malt."

He served Tony, then Owen and himself, and set a gravy boat filled with mushrooms seared in garlic and pepper beside me while he poured Cabernet. I helped myself, then passed the mushrooms to Owen, who took a spoonful and handed them to Tony. He continued talking with Tony all the while, until Julio resumed his seat, then picked up his knife and fork. Owen and Julio conducted the meal with a smooth precision I deeply admired. Usually a dinner this elaborate would be served by a butler—something I'd only experienced a couple of times myself. But between them, with only a little bending of conventions, our two hosts kept everything moving. There were no awkward pauses, and Julio never seemed rushed. He kept our glasses filled and managed to appear relaxed as he enjoyed his excellent handiwork.

The steak and the mushrooms were both perfectly prepared. There were no complicated sauces. They needed none. I was pleased to see Tony dig in with gusto, and more pleased when he remembered to compliment Julio.

"This is all really great," were his words. I made a mental note to tell Julio that while this didn't sound like high praise, it was rare to hear Tony comment on the quality of a meal.

Owen had either run out of questions about police work or was taking a breather. I took advantage of a moment's pause to thank him again for the photos, and tell him about Mr. Hidalgo's reaction to the copies I had given him.

"Wonderful," Owen said, smiling. "That makes it all worthwhile."

"Yes. Please remember to send me your bill."

A swift glance passed between Owen and Julio. "I will," Owen said. "This week has been a bit busy."

"Where did you learn to play the harp?" I asked after a brief silence. "Are you self-taught?"

"A combination of that and two years in high-school orchestra. I did take a few private lessons at first."

We chatted about music for a while. When everyone had finished the main course, Julio removed the plates and served a palate cleanser —a magnificent, subtle sorbet of lemon and rosemary—before bringing out the salad course. I was beginning to feel full, but the mercifully small mound of shaved radish and jicama tossed with microgreens and dressed with a light, citrusy vinaigrette, was the perfect dish to follow the steak.

I had just enough room for a couple of bites of dessert, and that was exactly what Julio provided: tiny slices of flourless chocolate torte, sprinkled with toasted piñon nuts and a light drizzle of salted caramel. The torte must have been no more than four inches in diameter. I glanced at Tony, wondering if he thought the portion too small, but he had his eyes closed and looked blissful, savoring the first bite.

Julio set a dessert plate at his own place, then went to the sideboard. "Ellen, may I offer you some port or sherry? There's whiskey or B and B, if you prefer."

"Port sounds lovely, thank you."

Tony opted for whiskey, and Owen chose Amontillado. Julio poured the same for himself and took his seat.

I cut tiny slices of chocolate torte with my

fork, alternating them with sips of port, occasionally picking up a piñon. I would not have
been able to eat a large portion, so I made the
small one last as long as possible. I couldn't help
wondering if this dessert might make a good
sweet for the tearoom, perhaps with an adjust-
ment to the caramel to make it less messy, but I
had resolved not to mention work to Julio that
evening.

"Magnificent meal, Julio. Thank you," I said.

Tony nodded enthusiastically, and raised his
glass. "Here's to the chef."

Julio bowed his head, smiling in bemusement
as Owen and I joined the toast. "Thank you," he
said, then picked up his own glass. "And here's
to your future happiness." He looked from me to
Tony as Owen joined the toast.

I smiled, meeting Tony's gaze. "Thank you."

"How did your house-hunting go?" Julio
asked.

I sighed. "No luck this week. We'll try
again."

Julio nodded, took a bite of torte, and glanced
at Owen.

"What about the kitten?" Owen asked. "Did
you find her a home?"

"Not yet. Send your cat-loving friends to me,
please."

He looked at Tony. "Do you like cats?"

Tony shrugged. "Mom always had them, until she moved to a place that doesn't allow them."

"Ah." Owen sipped his sherry.

I lifted my glass, found it nearly empty, and took a final sip, leaving a little in the bowl. Setting it down, I smiled with the satisfaction of finishing a delightful meal. A perfect meal, in fact.

I would have to reciprocate, which would take some ingenuity. Certainly I couldn't outdo Julio's cooking, and right now my only dining room was the one at the tearoom, probably not a relaxing venue for Julio. I toyed with the idea of putting a table in the upstairs hall for an evening, but it would be a bit of fuss and bother, and I'd have to serve from my little kitchenette. Better to wait until Tony and I had a place, perhaps.

Julio stood and began collecting the empty dessert plates. Roused from my musings, I looked at Tony, who was contentedly swirling the whiskey in his glass. He met my gaze and smiled. I smiled back, glad he was comfortable. Maybe he had decided Owen was all right. He could not have failed to notice the harmony between Owen and Julio.

"I can make coffee now, or leave it until a little later," Julio offered when he returned.

"Later, please," I said. "I'm sated."

"Would you care to take a short walk?" Owen

asked. "I'd like to show you something."

I glanced at Tony, who had just drained his glass. "Sure," I said, though I felt a temptation to just curl up on one of the sofas.

"I'll get coats," Julio said, and disappeared.

Owen took a final sip of his sherry, leaving a little in the glass as I had done. A quiet smile lingered on his lips. When Julio returned, Owen stood and helped me into my coat, then slid into a long, black wool coat that I thought I'd seen him wear at the tearoom once or twice. We stepped outside into the frosty night, our breath coming out in clouds as Owen and Julio led the way down the sidewalk toward the end of the street. Tony and I followed, my hand tucked into his elbow. Stars spangled the cold, dark sky.

I wondered if we were near the old star fort that had been built by the soldiers of Fort Marcy during the Civil War. It was somewhere on this hilltop, I knew. Was that what Owen wanted to show us?

Instead of ending, the street curved back toward the road. It was a loop, I realized. Right at the angle of the curve, Owen and Julio turned up the path of a townhouse on the south side of the street. Its driveway was empty, but the porch light was on, gleaming through a crescent-moon cutout. Owen produced a ring of keys and unlocked the front door, then turned to us.

"Come in. Have a look at this place and see if you like it."

He went in and turned on lights. It was empty, his footsteps echoing on the tile floor. The design was similar to his and Julio's place, but not identical. They were clearly part of the same development, but in this house, the living room was straight ahead. I could see Santa Fe through its picture window even from the front door. Breathtaking.

"Is it yours?" I asked, scarcely daring to hope.

"Yes. Inherited from my parents." Owen walked into the living room and turned to face us as we followed. His mouth twisted in a wry smile. "I'm afraid I'm one of those dreadful trust children. Please don't hold it against me."

"Of course not," I said immediately. My brain was still processing the information, though it didn't surprise me. I'd been right that he didn't need to work for a living.

"I do try to use my blessings to assist others. Until lately, Roberto and Gwyneth lived here."

"Oh!"

Roberto was an artist, a former rival of Gabriel's. I remembered Julio mentioning that he and the vivacious Gwyneth had recently moved, due to Roberto's success in the art community.

"I'd like to offer it to you two, if you're

interested." Owen raised a hand, forestalling protests. "The rent doesn't matter. Make it whatever feels right to you. I donate all rental proceeds to charity."

"We can't afford what it's worth," Tony said bluntly. "You could make more."

"Yes, but I don't *need* more. I'd much rather have pleasant neighbors and lend a bit of a hand to some friends. Can't let the vacationers have all the good views, after all."

"Oh, Owen," I said, "that's amazingly generous of you! I don't know what to say."

"Don't say anything yet. Have a look around, make sure it suits you. You can bring the kitten, by the way, but you'll have to keep her inside. We see coyotes now and then."

I glanced at Tony, then at Julio, who was watching from the entryway. He smiled. "Come and see the kitchen."

I followed him, leaving Tony and Owen behind in the living room. I could hear them talking in low voices. Hope had begun to rise in my heart, but I knew Tony's pride would make it hard for him to accept such a gift.

The kitchen was spacious, with a center island, double sink, and all-new appliances including a double oven, the topmost being narrow, ideal for a pizza or a sheet of cookies.

Or scones.

"Oh, I love this!" I cried, opening its door and peering in.

"Here's the best part," Julio said, beckoning me to the back of the kitchen. He opened what looked like a closet door, revealing a walk-in pantry cupboard, lined with shelves.

"Oh, fabulous!" I stepped in, turning a full circle. I could reach almost every shelf.

"There's even an outlet, in case you want to bring in a wine cooler. Some of the shelves are removable."

"You and Owen have a wine cooler, I'm sure."

"Two. He's a connoisseur. I'm learning a lot."

I turned to look at him. "I'm so happy for you, Julio."

"Thanks," he said softly. "I'm really happy, too."

"Don't quit on me until I can find...the impossible. Someone who can replace you."

"I have no intention of quitting. I'd go crazy without something to do. And anyway, I want to make a name for myself."

I rejoined him in the kitchen. "In Santa Fe? I don't think the tearoom will do it for you."

He closed the pantry door and leaned against the island. "The tearoom's a beginning. We've had good reviews so far, and a couple have even mentioned my name."

"What about your art? You could paint now, if you wanted."

"I thought about it. But I think I'd rather be a famous Santa Fe chef." He grinned.

"Well, the meal you gave us tonight was a *tour de force.* And by the way, thank you for adapting to Tony's tastes. Meat and potatoes, indeed."

Julio chuckled. "I wondered if you'd notice."

"It was the best meat-and-potatoes meal ever. With chocolate cake for dessert, even."

Julio threw his head back, laughing. "Guilty."

"You should make it a *prix fixe,* when you move up. It'll be a hit." I leaned against the counter opposite him. "I have no doubt you can be famous, but you'll have to have your own restaurant."

He nodded. "I'm still learning, for now. And I will never abandon you. I'm keeping my eye out. Actually, Hanh is a possibility to run the tearoom in a couple of years."

I nodded. "I'm terrified of her, though."

Julio chuckled. "Don't be. She's a marshmallow under all that Asian discipline."

"Is she?"

Footsteps approached, and Owen came into the kitchen, followed by Tony. "I knew you'd get stuck in here. Take a look at the bedrooms before you decide."

"Bedrooms? Plural?"

"Two, and two baths. Sixteen hundred square feet."

Wow. A palace, compared to my suite, or to Tony's place. Bigger than both combined, actually.

I looked at Tony as we followed Owen down the hall to admire the rest of the house. He wasn't glowing with delight, but he seemed resigned.

We paused to glance in at a laundry room with another double sink. Joy!

The bedrooms were ample, with a walk-in closet in the master bedroom and French doors overlooking the city view. Outside, I spotted a covered hot tub in a small yard enclosed by a half-height adobe wall. Enough room for a little gardening.

"Well, it's a dream as far as I'm concerned," I said, turning hopeful eyes to Tony.

He met my gaze. It wasn't what he'd hoped for, because it wasn't something we could do on our own. But why settle for less, when a friend was offering such a kindness?

"If you need some time to think about it, that's fine," Owen said. "There's no hurry."

Tony looked out at the amazing Santa Fe view. "No," he said, "that won't be necessary. We'll take it, and thank you."

I threw myself at Tony, wrapping my arms around him and evoking a masculine chuckle from one of the others. "Thank you," I whispered in his ear.

"Bravo!" Julio said. "Shall we go back for coffee now? It's chilly in here."

We paused in the front yard while Owen locked the door. I hugged Tony's arm. "Thank you for being willing to accept this gift," I murmured.

He turned to look at me, taking me by the shoulders. "You'll be safe here," he answered softly. "None of the places we looked at were as safe as this."

I hugged him, then slid my hand into his elbow as we fell in behind our hosts, soon to be our neighbors. A great weight of worry rose into the night sky along with our freezing breath, to be carried away on the wind, gone and soon forgotten.

About the Author

photo by Chris Krohn

PATRICE GREENWOOD was born and raised in New Mexico, and remembers when the Santa Fe Plaza was home to more dusty dogs than trendy art galleries. She has been writing fiction longer than she cares to admit, perpetrating over twenty published novels in various genres. She uses a different name for each genre, thus enabling her to pretend she is a Secret Agent.

She loves afternoon tea, old buildings, gourmet tailgating at the opera, ghost stories, costumes, and solving puzzles. Her popular Wisteria Tearoom Mysteries are colored by many of these interests. She is presently collapsed on her chaise longue, sipping Wisteria White tea and planning the next book in the series.

What's Next?

A Valentine for One

Wisteria Tearoom Mysteries #8

At a quarter to eleven on the first Tuesday in February, I stood at the hostess station in the Wisteria Tearoom's gift shop, attired in my best lace dress. A whisper of macaron aroma—sugar and almonds, with a hint of elderflower—reached me from the pastry case nearby, and I swallowed. I'd had a light breakfast in anticipation of my tea date that morning.

The macarons were featured on the February menu, debuting that day. Normally I would not have made a date to entertain a guest to tea until the menu had settled in for a few days, but this was a busy month and Tuesday was the quietest day of the week for us, usually. I trusted Julio to make sure the food was perfect, especially since my guest was his roommate (and partner), Owen Hughes.

The bells on the front door tinkled and I glanced toward the hall. Women's voices murmured in pleased tones. I looked at the reservations screen, checking for the name Olavssen out of habit. The Bird Woman was a top customer, and also a wild card. I was guiltily relieved to see that she did not have a reservation this morning.

Three ladies stepped into the gift shop: an older woman escorting two teens, their eyes gleaming with delight. Probably they'd gotten out of school to celebrate a birthday, I surmised from the gift bags carried by one of the teens. I barely had a chance to wish them good morning before Rosa, one of my servers, whisked them away to the main parlor.

My stomach rumbled. Resisting the urge to dash down the hall to the butler's pantry and grab a cup of tea, I prowled the gift shop, looking for things to straighten. They were in short supply this early in the day, but I managed to distract myself by rearranging the valentine cards.

"Choosing one for your fiancé?" asked Dale behind me. I glanced at him, taking in his dark gray vest and slacks, silvery satin dress shirt, and burgundy bow tie, all setting off his slightly rakish curling hair. Dapper as usual, and I loved the masculine touch he brought to the tearoom staff.

"Which one do you like best?" I countered. I'd already picked a card to give to Tony, but I was always interested in the male point of view.

"That one," he said without hesitation,

reaching past not only the flowery-hearty cards, but also the plaid and the scene of ducks that were there as more masculine offerings. His fingers tapped the top edge of a Mucha reproduction, a voluptuous woman in flowing pink silks, standing on tiptoe and looking coyly over her shoulder at the viewer, framed by an Art Nouveau crescent. Meeting my inquiring gaze, he added, "But then, I've always been partial to nymphs."

"A sign of excellent taste," remarked another voice. Owen's.

Dale and I both turned. Owen stood in the doorway, dramatically formal in a black morning coat with his long, dark hair loose over his shoulders, an elegant turquoise bolo tie the only touch of color about him.

CPSIA information can be obtained
at www.ICGtesting.com
Printed in the USA
BVHW070037141021
618896BV00004B/334